Return to Treasure Island

Jack Trammell

Inspired, read, edited, and the end co-authored by
Liberty Middle School Eighth Grade Students

Hard Shell Word Factory

The author would like to thank the staff and students of Liberty Middle School for their support and encouragement. In particular, the eighth grade class from 1997-1998 helped author with the ending, and provided great feedback during the completion of the book.

ISBN: 0-7599-0286-0

Electronic version published August 1999
Print published December 2000

Hard Shell Word Factory
PO Box 161
Amherst Jct. WI 54407
books@hardshcll.com
http://www.hardshell.com

Chapter 1

THE STORMS came more often this summer. They were intensified by ocean currents that blew violent tropical weather in from the south, and whenever they arrived Jonathan Cox was forced to stay inside and entertain himself with magazines and novels, or the math workbooks that his uncle forced him to complete.

Jonathan stared at the math workbook on the desk in front of him and frowned. Then he pushed it aside and gazed out the small oval window at the swirling surf and black clouds. In a way, he thought to himself, the storm outside was like his life the past half year—angry, a little out of control, and very unpredictable.

It had been exactly five months since his parents had left him. They had been on a plane that disappeared over some small islands in the Atlantic Ocean—the same mad, swirling ocean outside his window—leaving behind only a garbled radio message and some important Xeroxed papers in a safe that his mother's brother, Uncle Pinchbeck (formerly Osbourne, which he decided was too common a last name, and whom Jonathan was not allowed to call by his first name, Frank, anyway), had been extremely anxious about.

Jonathan did not accept it at first; had insisted that they would be back. They were probably stranded on one of the islands, or floating in a life raft somewhere waiting to be rescued. Jonathan had too many plans about becoming a young adult and exploring the world to lose the primary anchors in his life. Five months with his secretive, eccentric uncle, however, changed his mind. His parents were never coming back, and the reality of this finally took its full effect on him.

The lightning outside seemed to be striking the ocean itself. What was it actually hitting? he wondered. The lightning reminded him of the plane crash. What had hit the plane? The FAA people said it was probably a mechanical failure, but they never found any wreckage. It was as if the earth had swallowed the plane up. Or, perhaps lightning had struck it. It didn't matter, anyway, since his uncle never permitted anyone to talk about it.

Uncle Pinchbeck was a decent sort, Jonathan tried to admit, but he was almost fifty and had never been married or had any children himself, and his personality centered mainly around the preservation and growth of his enormous wealth. He always told Jonathan that the plane crash was ancient history, and that it was unhealthy to linger on it. His parents were gone, so he should get on with the business of life.

But aren't thirteen-year-olds supposed to miss their parents? Aren't they supposed to be concerned about the unknown future? Of course they are! he told himself.

The storm outside seemed to grumble in agreement.

"COME ON, Jonnie, eat up."

Uncle Pinchbeck was eating an elaborate salad that the cook had created with hearts of romaine and alfalfa sprouts, but he always had "kid" food prepared for Jonathan.

Jonathan toyed with the peas and carrots on his plate and studied his uncle. He was not a handsome man, although he did bear a striking resemblance to Jonathan's mother in his piercing greenish eyes and blond hair. He groomed himself meticulously which seemed to water down his personality. Even then, he certainly didn't look like a millionaire, or a person that teenagers would be thrilled to hang out with.

"If you don't eat your food, you won't grow up strong like me!" Uncle Pinchbeck liked to laugh at his own jokes.

Jonathan cringed. Why wouldn't his uncle admit that his nephew was thirteen, practically a young adult? Peas were not as important as independence.

"After the storm, I'm going out to the island to check on the buildings. I assumed you would be going with me."

"Yes, Uncle Frank."

A deep scowl passed over his face. "Pinchbeck. Remember?"

"Yes, sir."

"We'll maybe do a little fishing, if you want."

Jonathan rolled his eyes. "The fishing's not very good after a storm, Uncle."

"Oh, really? Hmm... I guess that's so. Well, anyway, we'll leave after dinner if it's clear enough."

"What were those papers in the safe about?" Jonathan asked suddenly.

Uncle Pinchbeck paused in mid-bite. This was not an approved topic. For some reason, he remained very sensitive about the mysterious papers. "Hmm? The, um, papers were to do with your parent's plans for you....That kind of thing. I'm taking complete care of it. Trust me, their wishes will be done; are being done."

"I'll bet they're copies of the—"

"Enough!" he said. "I told you to forget about the crash. The papers are not your business, and you need to quit asking about them."

"But my parents weren't on a vacation, like

you say they were. They would have told me that."

"They were on a vacation, Jonathan."

"But what if they're still alive somewhere? Wouldn't they want us to keep looking for them? Maybe the papers said something about—"

"Silence!"

With that, Uncle Pinchbeck got up and left the room, retreating to his den for a pipe smoke and the rest of the newspaper, with maybe a few phone calls or emails mixed in. He was in the real estate business—world-wide, in fact—and his money was growing so fast that he had no idea what he was really worth. Currently, his pet project was financing some shipbuilding company in Connecticut that made hulls for nuclear submarines. Uncle Pinchbeck was good at what he did, however, and Jonathan did have to concede that he was provided for.

His uncle was not a good parent, though. He restricted Jonathan from a normal social life by making him attend an elite private school near Savannah, confined him in the house on weekends, and coerced him into following his uncle around like an enthusiastic business apprentice. Uncle Frank Pinchbeck—(formerly Osbourne)—was no-thing like his sister, Hillary. Jonathan's mother had thrown slumber parties, taken all his friends with him skating and to the movies, gone on picnics, encouraged him to play sports....

But those days were over.

These were the dog days of summer in Georgia, and they were dog days for Jonathan, too. He flipped several of his peas onto the silk table cloth.

Why wouldn't Uncle Pinchbeck talk about the papers his mother had found? And how would Jonathan ever have a normal life again? These were two of the questions that rattled around his head all of the time.

More importantly, though, he also couldn't shake the strong feeling that his parents were still alive, and that he had to do something about it. The clues were hidden in the papers.

UNCLE PINCHBECK kept the papers under lock and key. They were actually nothing more than a torn corner of a map and some scrawled hand-writing on the outside of an old envelope. His mother found them in Jonathan's grandfather's attic when he died.

Jonathan's parents never told him exactly what the papers were all about, insisting that he was too young and might misunderstand them. But it was perfectly clear that they were interested in them, and from time to time Jonathan was able to catch a glimpse of the mysterious articles when his parents were holding a late night discussion after he was supposedly fast asleep.

He once heard his father, Lawrence, say, "And don't ever let your brother see this! He's crazy enough to change his name, for no apparent reason. He's also just crazy enough to..." And he couldn't catch the rest.

The papers were why they had left for the small island in the middle Atlantic, Jonathan was sure of it. Now, unless Uncle Pinchbeck changed his secre-tive habits, Jonathan might never know what the papers were really about, or why his parents had disappeared.

"MASTER COX, the phone is for you."

Longfellow, Uncle Pinchbeck's butler, chauffeur, and portfolio manager, handed the cordless phone to Jonathan. Longfellow was probably over seventy, but still had the unflappable dignity of a president or prime minister etched in the lines of his face.

"I believe it's Katherine, sir."

Jonathan put down his pencil at his desk and took the phone. Of course, Uncle Pinchbeck didn't allow him to have his own private phone in his room.

"Hello?"

"Hi, it's me, Katherine."

"Hi!"

Katherine was the only friend he had met in the neighborhood, since his school was mainly for rich boys from Savannah, and she lived with her father in a run-down house near the marina where Uncle Pinchbeck's boat was stored. Actually, it wasn't much of a house. Katherine's mother was dead; her father an alcoholic who didn't have much money since he worked only about half the year as a fisherman. It was something that she always felt she had to apologize for.

"You should see what the storm did over here," she said.

"I know, my Uncle's taking me to the island tonight to see the damage."

"Well, do you want to come over for a while before you go, and help me get my boat patched up? It rolled in the surf and there's a hole in the keel now."

"Sure. I'll be over in ten minutes."

THE WALK to Katherine's was about half a mile, following the rim of the bay in a gentle semi-circle as it weaved its way around Snake Point to the outer breaks and the local marina. Beyond that was the open sea. Jonathan made good time, watching the sun bravely try to overcome the final gusts of wind from the storm, walking swiftly along the sandy coastline and looking at the damage. This gale had been mild. There was some debris washed up, along with the inevitable smell of dead seaweed and other shore creatures killed. Hundreds of sea-gulls were calling loudly to one another, spreading the word about a sudden feast that had befallen them. Still, this was nothing like a real hurricane.

The marina was a bustle of activity as people arrived to check their boats for damage. Katherine waved to him from the beach on other side, then ran to him. She was wearing jeans that were torn and faded, and Jonathan knew better than to mention anything—it was like her family's house; something she was ashamed of.

Katherine was thirteen, too, with dirty blonde hair tied in a pony tail and just enough freckles to be cute, despite a lack of fashionable clothes.

"Hi, Jonathan. How are you?"

Jonathan gazed out across the open expanse of the Atlantic in the distance and sighed. "I'm okay."

"Thinking about your parents again?"

"Sort of."

Katherine moved closer and studied him like a mother. "You're not still insisting that they're out there somewhere, are you, waiting to be rescued? Not after this long."

Jonathan shrugged. "Robinson Crusoe lived a lot longer than that, didn't he?"

"That's only a book," Katherine said, rolling her eyes.

"A book..." Jonathan echoed.

"YOU CAN'T dwell on this forever, Jon. Trust me—it was the same with my mother. It hurts, but sooner or later you'll have to accept things. You only have a few more years until you can go out into the world on your own, anyway."

Katherine pointed over to the other side of the marina to a bright red boat that was larger than the others. "The creep brothers came out and checked the boat already. They left a few minutes ago. Think your uncle would mind if we go on board before we patch my boat?"

"I don't care what he thinks," Jonathan said, scowling.

The creep brothers were two of Uncle Pinchbeck's employees. They always drove his car, or the boat, or rode in the private plane he owned at the airport in Savanna.

Jonathan and Katherine hopped aboard the *Victory*, which was really more like a yacht, and pulled at the cabin door. It was unlocked. Down below, there was a roomy cabin, a bedroom which faced out on the water, and several small rooms which included a kitchen and bathroom. The cabin, along with numerous nautical antiques and arti-facts, included a large television. Jonathan turned it on while Katherine went into the kitchen, opened the refrigerator, then peered inside.

Above them was a large dining room, or "state" room as Uncle Pinchbeck called it..

"This is a cool boat," she said, still looking over the various items inside the fridge. "How come you hardly ever take me out in it?"

Jonathan shrugged and walked over to the bedroom door that always stayed locked. Just out of curiosity, he tried it. To his surprise, it fell open.

"Hey," Katherine said, "I've never seen in there."

Jonathan stepped inside slowly and surveyed the scene. In the back of the room, a rectangular window covered with blinds looked out on the ocean. There was also a small bed, a heavy navy-style chest of drawers with large round knobs, and a desk that folded out from the wall.

On the desk was a folder.

Jonathan moved towards it.

"Maybe we shouldn't be in here," Katherine said suddenly. "Your uncle might get really mad."

Jonathan ignored her and opened the folder. Inside were two pieces of paper—a torn piece of a map and an old envelope.

Chapter 2

"WHAT IS IT?" Katherine whispered.

Jonathan held the papers up and contemplated them for a moment, savoring the possibility of unraveling this one small mystery, but also frightened by the notion that he might be going against his parents wishes.

"They never wanted me to see these," he said.

"Who?"

"My parents. Remember I told you about the papers that sent them flying off? These are the papers."

Katherine reached over curiously, but Jonathan drew them back.

"What could it hurt now, Jonathan? Wouldn't they want you to know?"

"I don't know. They must have had legitimate reasons for not telling me."

"Go on, Jon, read it."

She was right, of course. If they were dead, it didn't matter. With only a brief moment's hesitation, he plunged into it, reading the letter out loud:

"To William Osbourne: Hello, my grandson. I

know if you are reading this it means that I have passed on. I'm sorry that I won't be able to fish with you anymore, or stroll through the back meadow like we used to, but I trust that you will do so with your grandson and remember me simply that way."

Jonathan paused and smiled. His Grandfather William had, indeed, taken him on many fishing trips on the James River. His great, great grandfather had been a fisherman, too.

"There are a couple of small matters that need to be taken care of. First, you have been told all your life that you are related to the writer, Stevenson. This is true, and I would find it extremely unusual if you haven't already become acquainted with a number of his works, including Treasure Island, which is undoubtedly the best known work. For the record, Stevenson was your great, great grandfather; he married my grandmother. If it's important, and you want to do a little genealogical digging, I'm sure the proof can be produced.

"However, the second matter is of a more serious nature. Your great grandfather (my father) told me before he died that many parts of T.I. were grounded in real events. For example, R.L.S. met the 'real' Long John Silver in an old tavern near Milford Haven over ten years before he wrote the actual book. He also told me that the island was

real, and that Silver entrusted him with the only real map to it. R.L.S. was a writer and an explorer, of course, but he was also sickly, so he never tried himself to find it. My father, whom you never knew, swore to me that it was not a hoax.

Now you know, Billy, that I have never been at a loss for a Pound or two if I needed it, but I turn what's left of this map over to you as your inheritance. Make of it what you will. I've heard that in America, where you're finishing school, they probably don't believe in such tales! But promise me this—if you ever find the treasure, throw a couple of Doubloons on my grave to let me know!

Take care of yourself. Signed: Grandfather (Deane Osbourne)."

Jonathan folded the letter back carefully, then turned to the map fragment.

"You're related to Robert Louis Stevenson?" Katherine said, in awe.

Jonathan ignored her. The map was of a small horseshoe shaped island. Scattered across it, all very crudely sketched, were several palm trees, a sunken ship, some squiggly lines, and a large X.

"Why wouldn't my parents tell me this?" Jonathan wondered out loud. "They threw away their lives on buried treasure!"

"Jonathan, I don't think you—"

A sudden noise on top of the boat caused them

both to jump. The creep brothers were back. Jonathan threw the papers back in the folder on the folding desk and pushed Katherine into the kitchen. The footsteps drew closer, so he changed plans and pulled her back into the bedroom where there was a large storage closet.

"Quick—get in here."

They pushed and shoved their way through life-jackets, aluminum poles, and white flags, and even each other. Jonathan quickly and quietly slid the closet door shut.

"Why are we hiding on your own boat?" Katherine hissed.

"Shh! I want to hear them."

The voices of the goons grew louder as they moved through the ship and then entered the bedroom.

"...Yeah, and Mr. Pinchbeck said to have the boat fully gassed and stocked, but the store was sold out of half the stuff he wanted. He must be going on a long trip this time."

"I'll bet he's going to that island, again."

"Maybe so. But he ain't going to be happy we didn't get the stuff. And why go by boat?"

"I don't know. Why do you think he's so interested in that island?"

"It's probably those papers—the ones over here—maybe that's the reason."

"I wouldn't touch those if I were you..."

In the closet, the air was growing stale and their limbs stiff. Jonathan heard the papers rustling.

"Look at this here—it's a treasure map!"

It was at that moment that the foam ring under Jonathan's backside chose to slide a little bit, and that caused the pile of lifejackets to shift, which then caused both Jonathan and Katherine to tumble out of the closet in a pile of equipment.

It was hard to say who was more shocked. Jonathan felt his face turning red.

"What are you two-ins doing here?" Graham, the larger of the two goons (and the dumber, Jon thought) said as he helped them up roughly and shoved the papers into his companion's hands. "Were you spying on us?"

Clarence, the other goon who was skinny and weasel-like, tried to put the map and envelope back discreetly. Jonathan saw him.

"What are you doing reading Uncle Frank's papers?"

Clarence shrugged and stabbed his finger at Jonathan. "The papers were just lying there for all to see. But you, both of you, were hiding in the clo-set. I think you are the ones with some explaining to do. And you'd better call him Pinchbeck, kid!"

"Explain what?" a voice boomed.

Uncle Pinchbeck lowered himself into the cabin and faced them all with an angry twitch on his lower lip.

"Would somebody like to explain what's going on here?"

Clarence smiled smoothly and walked toward the doorway and Uncle Pinchbeck. "We got most of the supplies you requested, but when we were loading them, we found these two hiding in the closet..."

"They were reading your papers," Jonathan said.

Uncle Pinchbeck's pock-marked face turned purple, and his upper lip joined the lower one in dancing. "All of you are out of line! Do I have to lock everything up around here? I can't even trust my own hired help and nephew!"

Uncle Pinchbeck threw his hands in the air and turned around to go topside. "Take us to the summer house," he said over his shoulder, "that's what I came out here to do."

"Yes, sir," Graham said, following him like a dog.

Clarence lingered behind, staring at Katherine and Jonathan and running a hand through his crew cut hair. "I'm going to tell you something, kid, and I want you to remember it. I don't care if Pinchbeck is your uncle! If you ever snitch on me again like that, I'll, I'll..." He frowned and snapped his fingers suddenly. “Figure it out!”

Jonathan shrank back from him as he walked away to join Graham.

“Jon, he can’t talk to you like that!” Katherine said in a whisper.

Jonathan didn’t say anything for several moments. Then he simply shook his head.

This was definitely not like the old days.

For some reason, he thought of Treasure Island. Clarence and Graham were like modern pirates. But what did that make Uncle Pinchbeck?

THE SUMMER house was a mansion in its own right. With seven bedrooms, two decks, a pier that ran from the house directly through a small lagoon to the Atlantic, and surrounded by lush vegetation, Uncle Pinchbeck had spared no expense.

Signs of the storm were evident, however. Many of the imported palm trees were down on the ground, and Uncle Pinchbeck hovered over one of them like it was a sick person.

“I can’t believe it,” he said in a low voice. “I paid over three-hundred bucks for each one of these.”

“They’re probably not dead,” Clarence said, bending over to inspect the shallow roots.

Jonathan and Katherine headed toward the house, which was built in modern style with lots of glass and white stucco walls. It appeared unharmed from the storm.

"Your uncle is weird," Katherine said.

Jonathan didn't respond. He was still thinking about the map and the letter. Was Robert Louis Stevenson really his great, great, great, great grandfather? That wasn't so hard to believe. Did his parents really believe the treasure of Long John Silver was there on that tiny island in the Atlantic? That was harder to believe. He did remember from the book, however, that Jim Hawkins and his friends had left the bar silver and the buried cache of arms on the Treasure Island.

Something had drawn his parents out there to the lonely stretches of the vast mid-Atlantic.

"Did you hear me, Jon?" Katherine said again.

"Yes. I was just thinking about this. Is my uncle's boat really large enough to sail the Atlantic?"

Katherine, Jonathan knew well, was well versed in the knowledge of ships and the sea. She had worked the nets with her father for years.

"Well," she began, "I'd say it is, but the *Victory* is definitely on the small side. I wouldn't sail the Atlantic this time of year in something so small."

"But they're going to."

Katherine's face darkened. "Jonathan, you're starting to do that thing again."

"What thing?"

"You know, when you get that look on your face like nothing is going to stop you."

Jonathan smiled. "I think you should go with me."

"No, no, no! It's too dangerous. Besides, your uncle would never agree to it."

"Who says Uncle Pinchbeck is going to approve?"

Katherine stopped while Jonathan unlocked the porch door at the side of the pier. Then they entered the darkened kitchen, which was bigger than Katherine's entire house.

"You're going to be a stowaway? On your uncle's own ship?"

Jonathan simply stared at her.

"I'm not going, Jonathan. It's crazy."

THE TRUTH was, Katherine didn't have much to keep her at home. Her father, while a good-souled man, was mired in the downfall of the fishing industry, and drank much too heavily to be a full-time father.

Her mother had passed away several years ago.

Katherine was logical, and sensible. It would take some serious convincing on the part of Jonathan. But she would be the perfect companion for an adventure.

"OKAY," JONATHAN said. "Here's what I'll do. You want to go to college, right?"

"Yes," she said slowly, reaching into the refrig-erator for an apple.

"And you told me money would be the big problem."

Katherine's gaze fell to the floor. Jonathan knew he was hitting a sore spot, but for a good cause.

"Katherine, come with me, and I promise I'll share half of the treasure."

"Jon, what if there is no treasure! And my father would kill me..."

"We could both leave home with that money and do whatever we want to."

For the first time, he saw a sliver of bright light come into her eyes. He knew that he was close to convincing her—crazy idea or not.

"We'll have to find a good place on the boat to hide, then store enough food and water for the trip. When we get to the island, we'll take the map from my uncle, find the treasure, then steal the boat back."

"And leave your uncle on the island?" she said, acting a little shocked.

"Yes," Jonathan said, smiling again.

"It is crazy!"

Jonathan nodded, but his face was completely serious now.

Chapter 3

LATER THAT night, Jonathan sneaked the portable phone into his room and shut the door. After dialing Katherine's number, a man's voice answered at the other end. Jonathan felt guilty talking to her father, knowing that she would be embarking on a trip that would upset him very soon.

After talking a moment about the storm, he brought Katherine to the phone.

"It's me," Jonathan said quietly. "Is it safe to talk?"

"Yes, he went downstairs now."

"I found out that they're leaving tomorrow morning. Tonight, Uncle Pinchbeck fed me this line about how I needed to visit the new school I'm going to this fall for the ninth grade, and how they have these great dormitory accommodations. He wants me to stay there for a few days."

"But school's not in session."

"I know. It's the stupidest thing I've ever heard of. But it's obvious he's trying to get rid of me for a few days. He made this big fuss about calling the airport and getting his plane serviced and ready, but it was just for my benefit. I spied on the goons again and heard them saying the *Victory* leaves at seven tomorrow morning. They're going to the island."

"Do you really think we can do this?"

"Of course! How do you think Jim Hawkins did it? He was younger than we are, and he even fought pirates."

Katherine chose not to say anything to that, although he could imagine clearly her face expressing disagreement. She was always skeptical of anything that went against the wishes of adults, but beyond that caution, she would be cool and calm in any difficult situation. She was a good friend, and she wouldn't have to be around her father's de-pressing life for a few days. It might be good for her.

"Well, make sure you bring a copy of Treasure Island," Jonathan said, ignoring her skepticism. "It may have some more clues in it that we'll need. I just read it last year in school, but I don't remember it all."

"I don't have a copy. This is crazy, Jon."

"Meet me at the boat in one hour. Can you sneak out?"

There was no answer, but Jonathan knew that he had her hooked. Katherine was the cautious type, but unavoidably curious, as well.

THE BOAT was locked, of course, but Jonathan pulled a surprise out of his pocket—a glittering key shaped like a small golden fork.

"Uncle Pinchbeck keeps spare keys in his vault—hundreds of them—but this was the only gold one. I saw it the other day."

He pushed it into the galley door and it turned smoothly. Moments later, they hauled several book bags of supplies down the narrow stairs and began unloading them.

Their hiding place was a storage room behind the stairs that served as a small access hall to the pumps and engine bilge. It was seldom, if ever, frequented during most journeys—the *Victory* being mostly a show-piece of wealth—and the door leading to it stayed closed and could even be locked from the inside in an emergency.

"Are we going to stay here the rest of the night?" Katherine asked.

"No, that's too suspicious. We need to go back and meet here at five."

"That's only four hours of sleep."

"Yes. But we've got to beat the goons. Help me put the rest of this stuff behind that crate in case they come in here for some reason before we do."

When everything was stowed safely, there remained but one last task. Jonathan rushed into

Uncle Pinchbeck's bedroom and hurriedly dug around until he found the papers again. As fast as he could, he copied both the map and the letter, then replaced everything exactly as it had been before.

Then, they re-locked the galley door and rushed home. Jonathan had nothing to worry about—his window beside the trellis he climbed down was open and ready for his return. No one in the house had stirred since he left.

FIVE IN THE morning came more quickly than Jonathan would have liked. The watch on his wrist was beeping beside his ear, and he had to stretch his other arm over to turn it off. The watch reminded him of his purpose behind the upcoming journey. If his parents were still alive, which some gut instinct told him they were, then time was running out for them. If they were stranded on the island, then they probably were desperate for food and water.

The fleeting thought occurred to him that his uncle would probably take care of them if he found them, since he was going to the island, too. But would he even look for them? After all, it was his own sister who was missing. Trusting Uncle Pinch-beck, however, was not something Jonathan could bring himself to do.

Jonathan grabbed several small items he had

forgotten before, including his toothbrush, a small flashlight, a pocket knife his father had given him, and a copy of Robert Louis Stevenson's, "Treasure Island." He shoved all but the book into his short's pockets.

Longfellow was already up, and he regarded Jonathan with muted surprise as he entered the main hallway upstairs.

"The Master is up rather early this morning, is he not?"

"Big day, Longfellow. I'm supposed to go see my new school, and I promised Katherine I would help her mend some nets first."

Longfellow nodded. "We'll, breakfast isn't ready yet, but you know where the cereal is if you want some."

"Thanks."

Jonathan skipped every other stair and flew through the kitchen. Unfortunately, his uncle was there, peeking over his wire-rimmed reading glasses and a cup of black coffee.

"Jonnie! Up so early? And in a hurry! Slow down for a second."

Jonathan reluctantly came to a halt and turned half way around. Uncle Pinchbeck set his mug down and stood up.

"Where are you off to? We've both got big trips today."

Jonathan fidgeted his feet nervously. "I know. I'm looking forward to visiting my school, but I need to see Katherine first. We wanted to test the repairs on her boat.

Uncle Pinchbeck looked at him suspiciously. "Well... Don't be very long, and if you see Clarence and Graham on my boat, tell them to get back here—I need to talk to them before we leave. And don't be long! If I'm late dropping you off, I'll be late for my appointment in New York."

"New York?"

"Yes, er, somewhere near there. An unscheduled crisis in one of the branch offices."

"So you're going to New York?"

Jonathan couldn't stand to listen to his uncle lie. His cronies were preparing the boat for a trip and he was pretending Jonathan couldn't understand what was going on? He decided to make Uncle Pinchbeck squirm a little bit.

Uncle Pinchbeck tightened his robe and straightened his glasses, then smiled. "Yes... New York... Now run along and see your little friend before we have to go. But I don't want Longfellow getting a speeding ticket again, and you know I'll leave when the time arrives. Don't be late getting back here."

"Yes, sir."

"By the way," Uncle Pinchbeck said suddenly. "What's that book in your hand?"

Jonathan held it up slowly, realizing too late that it was a damaging clue about his plans.

"Uh, Treasure Island. Katherine is going to borrow it. But I finished the math book, you'll be glad to know!"

Uncle Pinchbeck nodded slowly and sat back down, still staring at him as he ran out. His face looked a little bit like a lemon slice that had sat out in the sun too long.

WHEN THEY reached the *Victory*, the sun was just beginning to peek over the red horizon.

"Red in morn," Katherine began to chant, "sailors take warn."

Jonathan used the stolen key again to open the door. There was no sign of the goons, yet, which was curious. Jonathan decided they were probably sleeping in.

They each had their hands full of things they had forgotten on the first trip. Katherine had a toothbrush, like he did, and had also chosen another Robert Louis Stevenson book for entertainment: "Dr. Jekyll and Mr. Hyde."

Inside the access space, they settled in to wait for the journey to begin. They didn't dare turn any lights on the boat on, so Jonathan used the flash-light.

"Did you bring extra batteries?" Katherine

asked.

Jonathan didn't reply. Katherine produced an extra flashlight and batteries from her pile of gadgets. Then Jonathan pulled his book forward and began reading a section of, "Treasure Island," out loud. Katherine's brown eyes looked black and enormous across from him as he read to her.

"...There fell out the map of an island, with latitude and longitude, soundings, names of hills and bays, and inlets, and every particular that would be needed to bring a ship to a safe anchorage upon its shores. It was about nine miles long and five across, shaped, you might say, like a fat dragon standing up, and had two fine landlocked harbors, and a hill in the center part marked 'the spyglass.' There were several additions of a later date, but above all, three crosses of red ink—two on the north part of the island, one in the south-west, and, beside this last, in the same red ink, and in a small, neat hand, very different from the captain's tottery characters, these words: 'Bulk of treasure here.'"

Jonathan closed the book and sighed.

"He doesn't give the exact coordinates in the book, does he?" she asked.

"I don't think so. But the description of live oaks and pine trees and wild goats make it seem pretty temperate. Probably in the mid-Atlantic, somewhere not completely tropical."

"Do you think that letter from your great, great grandfather is real?"

"Yes. And my granddad and parents did, too."

"Well," Katherine shrugged, "we'll find out."

At that moment, a loud bang topside on the yacht caused them both to lapse into silence.

"Here we go," Jonathan whispered. "Gang way!"

Chapter 4

THEY LISTENED carefully for what seemed like an hour, but never once did they hear Uncle Pinchbeck's voice mixed in the conversation topside. Clarence and Graham were both hard at work readying the ship, and as expected, fighting amongst themselves.

Once, they came downstairs and rummaged through Uncle Pinchbeck's desk, and Jonathan was tempted to jump out and yell at them again. The moment passed, though, and the creeps returned topside.

"That Clarence gives me the creeps," Katherine whispered. "Why does your uncle tolerate someone like that?"

"Why does he tolerate either of them?" Jonathan replied. "For as much money as Uncle Pinchbeck has, you'd think he'd hire someone with a college degree and a little bit of common sense."

"No one with common sense would work for him," Katherine said, then quickly adding, "I mean, just that, well, he's a tough boss."

"I know what you mean, and you don't have to protect my feelings."

The *Victory* suddenly jerked free of her moorings, and the gentle sway of the bay rippled through the floor.

"Why didn't your uncle get on?"

"I don't know. Maybe we didn't hear him. Maybe he really went to New York and left Longfellow in charge of me when I didn't show up on time."

Had Uncle Pinchbeck been telling the truth about the business in New York? It still didn't seem likely. Why was the ship sailing, then?

The storage room they were hiding in was not nearly as uncomfortable as the closet they hid in previously, and a vent in the wall would provide fresh, tangy sea air if they needed it. They had food, water, entertainment, etc. The only problem was—

"Jonathan, I'm sorry, but I've got to go."

—How to use the bathroom.

"I was thinking about going up to investigate," he said, rising slowly and shoving his book bag and other things to the wall. "Why don't you go before I do that?"

"Just wait a minute. I'm going up with you."

"Kath, there's not room on the steps for both of us. And what if they catch me? They still won't know you're down here."

"Give them a little more credit than that, Jon,

even if they are dumb."

"Okay, okay, you're right, but it's safer for just one. You go ahead, and then I'll go up when you come back. I promise I'll be careful."

She scurried out the open hatchway, and reappeared only moments later.

"The coast is clear, Jon. Let's go."

He picked up "Treasure Island" and handed it to her. "Why don't you start reading this? Only one person should be put at risk."

She shrugged and sighed, obviously not satisfied, but willing to compromise on this occasion. As he left, she was holding the small flashlight in her teeth and flipping the pages open.

Jonathan carefully opened the hatchway to the cabin again and peered around the stairs. From his angle of sight, no one was visible in the outer cabin. The doors to the bedroom, small kitchen and bathroom were shut tight, and the only light in the room came from the rectangular windows next to the door at the top of the stairs. The huge antique pilot's wheel threw shadows into the corner where the day before Uncle Pinchbeck had stood and yelled at all of them.

With the gentle noise of water rushing by the moving boat, he could no longer clearly hear the voices above. Taking one step at a time, he inched his way up the slip-proofed steps until he could barely see out the left window, closest to the pilothouse. The other sizable room on the ship was behind a wall to his back, on the top level—a great room that stretched the length of the ship and housed a giant table with enough chairs to accommodate a dozen or more guests. It also had a pool table, a bar, and two televisions.

The goons were in the pilothouse, a small ten foot square structure that sat directly above their hiding place and was the highest part of the deck. They were bickering about something, but Jonathan couldn't hear anything since two walls were be-tween them.

There was, however, no sign what-so-ever of Uncle Pinchbeck, so perhaps he had gone to New York. Longfellow—poor man—would be looking for Jonathan everywhere. Disappointed, Jonathan made his way slowly back to their hiding place.

"He's not there," Jonathan said quietly upon rejoining Katherine in the dim artificial light.

"I already know," Katherine said.

Jonathan stared at her freckled face and she smiled triumphantly. After a moment's enjoyment of his confusion, she reached behind her and opened the vent in the wall. Ghostly voices drifted down to them in perfect timbre.

Jonathan smiled, too. He could hear every word the goons were speaking.

"Are we gonna be able to get Yankees games

out here on the t.v.?" Graham said.

"Fat chance," Clarence replied, "you'll be lucky to get the weather channel, since you don't know how to tune the dish."

"You're funny, Clarence, real funny. What do you want me to do—agree to take half your watch up here in return for tuning the stupid television in?"

"Actually, that sounds reasonable. You know me—I got no interest in the boob tube. I brought plenty of books. If you want me to take valuable time to tune the dish, well, you've got to return the favor."

Katherine shut the vent switch and smiled again.

"Listen to this, Jon. I heard them say that your uncle is flying his plane to the island. He came and got something from them right before we cast off."

"The letter and map," Jon said slowly, nodding.

"He wants the goons to meet him there with the *Victory*, so he can send the goods back by sea, instead of air."

"Goods?"

"That's the exact word they used." Katherine hesitated. "Do you think that means the treasure?"

Jonathan shrugged. So Uncle Pinchbeck had lied. Why did that not surprise him? And what did 'goods' mean?

"They act as if they've been to this island before..." Jonathan said half aloud. If Uncle Pinchbeck was flying to the island, then he had to know he could land there. He wouldn't start out without knowing that for a certainty. Or, perhaps, there was an island with an airstrip close by.

Maybe if his parents were still alive, which his heart told him must be true, then Uncle Pinchbeck might not want to find them on the island. That was a frightening thought.

Jonathan shook his head. No one could be that cruel to their own sister.

Katherine had her nose back in the book. Her voice carried over the pages around her face, which was silhouetted like a ghost by the light below. "You're a lot like Jimmy Hawkins, my lad," she said, spoofing Long John Silver. "I'm willing to bet they'll make you a sea dawg, yet."

He smiled back at her and suddenly thought of her own father. Drunk or not, he would be worrying about her soon. What they were doing would be a terrible shock to him. Longfellow, too, would be sick with worry.

"We should have left a note for your dad," Jonathan said slowly.

The smile vanished from her face like the sun passing behind the clouds. "He'll get over it, Jonathan. It's no big deal."

She buried herself back in the book.

"You're a little like Jim Hawkins, too," he said quietly, the anxiety still a little evident in his voice.

It was too late to turn back.

Chapter 5

THE FIRST two days went off without a hitch. Actually, they were highly productive days, since they learned more about the island by eaves-dropping on the goons' conversations, and also learned more about Uncle Pinchbeck's questionable business ventures.

"This'll be a big one," Graham had said. "More money than you or I will ever hope to stash away."

Clarence had only grunted in reply.

Both nights, the goons slept in the bedroom downstairs, which limited the forays Jonathan and Katherine could make out of the somewhat claustrophobic hiding space. But neither Clarence, nor Graham (who was the more mechanical of the two, it seemed, and would make the basic repairs) showed any inclination to stray near the hatch that led to the engines and pumps and also housed two very bored stowaways.

Katherine finished "Treasure Island" the first day, and was almost through with "Dr. Jekyll and Mr. Hyde."

They discussed the former book at length,

com-paring and contrasting it to their current adventure.

"Even if the pirate told your great how-many-ever-it-is grandfather the story of the treasure, how did he know that the old bugger wasn't just making up a tall tale?"

"I don't know. But Robert Louis Stevenson was no dummy. He wouldn't have lied about it to his own stepson, and he wouldn't have made anything up if it was going to be part of a legacy to his family."

"But how do you know it was a intentional legacy?"

"Grandfather William wouldn't have kept it if it wasn't real."

"But what if *his* grandfather just made it up?"

"You're confusing me," Jonathan complained, closing his eyes. "Too many generations. Why can't you just accept it?"

Katherine stared at him for a long moment. "How did Jim Hawkins know the treasure was real?"

Jonathan opened his eyes and sat up. He thought he could see where she was going. "He knew because of all the pirates—they wouldn't be willing to kill unless the treasure was real."

"Exactly!" Katherine said. "And think about the others—Dr. Livesey, and the Squire—they were willing to risk everything for it, too. Ask this now: who is willing to risk everything today?"

Jonathan nodded slowly.

"The treasure must really be there," he finally said.

Katherine nodded in agreement.

In the back of his sleepy mind, Jonathan remembered that the trip meant something entirely different to her than it did to him. She was smart, but dirt poor, and the treasure might be the only ticket to college. It might mean help for her father. Perhaps a newer, better boat; a way off the whiskey. He gazed in her direction and saw that she was smiling with her eyes closed. He could imagine some of the things she was dreaming about. When he closed his eyes, he could clearly see the image of his parents.

THEIR TRIPS outside of the access area became more bold as the trip wore on. While Clarence and Graham bickered amongst themselves, gorged on junk food, watched t.v. (despite Clarence's pronouncement that he was going to educate himself by reading), and generally were shiftless, Katherine and Jonathan came and went as they pleased below the deck, using the bathroom when necessary, skimming soda out of the fridge, or sneaking small food items out of the cabinets. Once, Jonathan was even so bold as to turn the t.v.

on, but nothing was coming in, and Katherine quickly made him turn it off.

"How long do you think it'll take to reach the island?" Jonathan asked her that evening, when they were truly confined due to the dangerously close sleeping quarters of the goons.

"I don't know exactly, but I'd guess at least six or seven days, and maybe more if it's truly in the eastern Atlantic near all the well-known islands."

It had been three days. Jonathan was really getting bored.

"I could use some excitement," he said, more than a trace of irritation in his voice.

"Be careful what you wish for," Katherine began sleepily.

"I know, or you just might get it. Not much chance."

"Do we have a way of doing any laundry? I'm almost out of clean clothes."

"I don't know. Maybe I can sneak out and do it tomorrow. There are mini machines hidden in the kitchen cupboards."

"Okay. I just don't want to start stinking."

"Maybe we should take showers."

"That's probably too risky."

"I guess so. Goodnight, Katherine."

"Goodnight, Jon."

Chapter 6

ON THE FIFTH day, they were too bold. It happened when Jonathan decided that washing the laundry had become an absolute necessity. In the friendly confines of the access area, the scents had grown a little like a locker room at a middle school, even with the vent open. Katherine was as embar-rassed as he was, and neither could really discuss it without blushing. Finally, Jonathan just grabbed the pile of clothes and tip-toed into the kitchen.

He did not hear Graham come in behind him.

"Hey, grab me a b—"

The words weren't out of Graham's mouth before each of them stopped in shock. Jonathan dropped the pile of dirty clothes at the same time that Graham's stubble-crusted jaw fell. Jonathan started to squirm by him, but Graham recovered, and was definitely not deficient in the physical strength department.

"What have we got here?" he said loudly. "Hey, Clarence! Get down here!"

Graham had Jonathan hooked by the shirt collar, and his hot breath poured all over

Jonathan's face. It smelled a little like the ocean and dead fish.

Clarence appeared moments later. His eyes glinted dangerously when he recognized the captive.

"Well, well, if it isn't the boss's son. Fancy meeting you out here. Taking a little vacation?"

Jonathan was too frightened to answer. For some reason, he was convinced that Clarence might be the type to just throw him overboard without any discussion, boss's son or not.

"I'll bet his little girlfriend's with him," Graham said, looking around the cabin, but refusing to let go of Jonathan's shirt, which was stretched to twice its normal proportions.

Jonathan finally managed words. "She's not here," he said, forcing confidence into his voice. "I came by myself because I wanted to get away from the prep school my uncle is so concerned I attend."

Clarence raised a crooked eyebrow and shook his head two different directions. "Oh, really?"

Jonathan nodded quickly.

"Then what is this?"

Clarence pointed down at the scattered laundry and several articles that obviously did not belong to a teenage boy.

"I'll search the boat from tip to tip," Graham said, shoving Jonathan at Clarence.

Clarence glared at him. "You mean, bow to

stern, and get started now! This was a stupid move, kid. Shark bait is the word. Or maybe a walk on the plank!"

At that moment, Clarence, the weasel-like handy man for a millionaire, with slicked back hair and beady eyes, suddenly took on the apparition of a old age pirate, complete with eye patch, sword, and cutlass, and a laugh that curdled blood.

"WELL," KATHERINE said, "at least they didn't throw us to the sharks."

"You mean, not yet."

Jonathan tugged at the cords that bound them, but there was no give. In fact, the more he pulled, the tighter they seemed to grow. Clarence and Graham had obviously made this type of knot before.

They were back to back, bound with part of a common strap, and several others individually as well, trapped against the wall in the bedroom near the closet. They could not see each other, and to make matters worse, they still were in their dirtiest clothes, having anticipated a change that never occurred.

"Is that you or me?" Jonathan said, wrinkling his nose, but Katherine didn't laugh. In fact, he felt a strange twitching against him that he soon dis-covered was caused by her quiet crying.

"I'm sorry," he said. "You were right when you said this whole thing was crazy. I should have listened to you."

Her crying stopped after a few minutes.

"We could get in a lot of trouble for this," he continued. "We'll probably be grounded for months. In fact, my uncle will probably send me to some private school in California, just to spite me. But I promise you this, Katherine. If we get to that island, we will get the treasure."

She surprised him by replying in a strong voice, as if she hadn't been crying at all.

"Let me ask you something, Jon. Do you think we're smarter than the goons?"

"Of course. But how does that help?"

She leaned her head back until it was touching Jonathan's back. "Look around us carefully. There's got to be something we can use to untie the straps."

Jonathan nodded and started looking.

"And Jon, one other thing—you really do stink."

He smiled in spite of himself.

AS THEY searched the room with their eyes, Jona-than didn't even realize the weather was changing. He was so engrossed in his task, that he didn't notice the light die down inside the cabin, despite the early afternoon hour. He had also grown so accustomed to the ceaseless swells that he paid no attention when they grew longer and steeper.

He did notice, however, that Katherine had stopped talking again. Her face, which he could barely see in a mirror on the wall, was listless and forlorn, like one of those people in a medieval painting that carry no emotion at all; very ashen and pale.

"Kath, are you all right?" he whispered, pulling fruitlessly at the ropes.

"Why does there always have to be a storm?" she said, her eyes still watery and unfocused.

"What are you talking about?"

"Can't you feel it? This boat's much too small... And every ocean adventure story has to have a storm in it. There's always one!"

"Well," Jonathan replied slowly, "the Hispaniola probably wasn't much bigger than this, and it weathered some pretty harsh weather."

Katherine met his eyes in the mirror. "This boat was not built for trans-Atlantic crossings, Jon, and the goons are not seafaring men."

"I haven't heard them worrying about anything."

"Exactly! Can't you feel it, Jon?"

Jonathan grew quiet himself and measured the growing width and breadth of every swell. Each one seemed to last an eternity, as if the boat were slowly climbing a great mountain.

"We're in big trouble, Jon."

Chapter 7

THE ONLY tool within possible range of grasping was a short piece of strap with a clip on the end that had fallen off a life jacket. Clarence and Graham had used a half dozen of the straps to restrain them. Jonathan started reaching for the stray strap, his fingers closing to within several inches of it.

"Quit pulling so hard!" Katherine complained. "What are you trying to do?"

"Quiet, please! I'm trying to get this other strap."

"Great," she whispered, "another piece of rope will really help untie all the other ropes."

Jonathan ignored her and continued inching closer and closer to the strap. When she coordinated her movements with him, they could slide a little further across the floor with each attempt. As he got close, a larger than normal swell caused them to slide further away, and Jonathan's angry words were echoed by shouts up on the deck. There really was a storm, and apparently the goons were now worried.

He worked again towards the strap, and finally, after straining every muscle, picked it up with his fingers and gave his aching neck a break, which had been twisted beyond normal limits to keep track of his target.

"Got it!" he said.

There was a loud bang above, and more cursing and shouting. The boat was beginning to pitch cra-zily, like a toy in a tub.

"We're not going to make it." Katherine said to herself.

Jonathan felt his way along the strap. At the very end, where the clip was attached, was a small, narrow plastic hook that locked the other end of the clip inside. With minimal effort, he bent the hook back and forth several times until it snapped off. Then he used the sharp end of it to pry between the layers of the knot behind Katherine's hands.

"What are you doing?" she asked.

"Did your mom ever have to get a knot out of your shoelaces?"

Moments later, the ropes fell free from her hands. She rubbed her raw wrists, then quickly un-tied his own hands. It was now difficult to stand up, due to the violent pitch of the boat, and water poured down the steps every few seconds.

"We need a plan," Katherine said.

He responded by handing her a lifejacket, then putting one on himself. He also tied a long strap to each one of them.

"You're the most sea-experienced hand we have, Kath. I'm going to distract the goons, and then I want you to sneak into the pilothouse and lock the door behind you. Take control and steer us out of the storm. Radio for help with your other hand, if you can do it at the same time. While you do that, I'll take care of the goons."

"Now this is crazy," she said.

Jonathan reached around her and hugged her as the floor suddenly dipped beneath them, causing them both to tumble to the floor. More water gushed down the stairs.

"Come on!" he shouted, picking her up. "It's got to be now!"

They climbed the stairs one at a time, slowly, fighting the wild movements of the boat. Lightning flashed periodically, throwing a strange ethereal white light over everything. Near the top, Jonathan could see where the goons were in the pilothouse arguing. As they yelled and pushed each other, the pilot wheel spun crazily, uncontrolled. Jonathan signaled for Katherine to conceal herself next to the pilothouse door.

"Tie off!" he said over the roar of the storm. "I don't want you washing over!"

She nodded quickly, then dashed across the deck to the pilothouse during the trough of the next swell. She quickly tied off on the rail and crouched down, so that anyone in the pilothouse would not be able to see her. Then she signaled him she was ready.

"Hey!" Jonathan began yelling, waving his arms back and forth. "Hey, you goons, we got loose! Just wait until I tell my uncle about this! Hey!"

At first they didn't seem to hear him, but a few seconds later, some sixth sense or something made Clarence look out the window and he spotted Jonathan jumping up and down wildly at the cabin entranceway. He immediately rushed for the door and collided with Graham, who had fallen off balance right into his path.

Jonathan turned to run back down the stairs just as both goons stumbled out the door and came after him. He didn't see it, but he could see in his mind how Katherine would quickly be getting up, untying herself from the rail, then rushing into the pilothouse and locking up behind her.

It was a good plan... At least the part about Katherine. Jonathan's part was suddenly more of a problem. When he reached the bottom of the stairs, he realized that he had no clue what to do.

"I've had enough of you," Clarence muttered, pausing on the stairs to pull something out of his back pocket. When a flash of lightning illuminated the cabin for a split second, Jonathan saw it was a knife—a long, gleaming fillet knife used by fishermen. Behind Clarence, Graham was pushing into him, whimpering about the storm.

"We're gonna die, Clarence! Go steer the ship! We're gonna die!"

"Shut up!" Clarence roared, shoving his free el-bow back into Graham's rather pouchy gut, which caused the large man to fall to the stairs to catch his breath. Clarence advanced slowly with the knife.

Jonathan felt around him. Some of the straps were still on the floor near the door, and some of them were longer than others. He reached frantical-ly until he found the longest one, then scrambled through the half-open bedroom door.

"You can't hide!" Clarence screamed.

The pitch of the boat caused the door to slam shut momentarily. Jonathan ripped his lifejacket off and then took the long strap and tied it around the heaviest thing he could find, which turned out to be a paper weight on the desk shaped like the boat. He experimentally swung the boat around like a sling and decided it was heavy enough.

When Clarence came through the door, Jonathan was ready. He swung the paper weight in a wide arc, connecting with Clarence's face right about at the temple. He went down like a rock. A second later, Graham stumbled through and looked in shock at Jonathan. He raised the sling again, but Graham cowered.

"Don't hit me with that thing. I won't hurt you, kid!"

"Tie him up," Jonathan ordered.

Graham reluctantly bent down to the task and never saw the blow that knocked him out cold, too.

IN THE PILOTHOUSE, things were not going so well. When Jonathan rejoined Katherine there, the storm had reached its peak of fury.

"It's no good, Jon! I can't keep it straight. The waves keep drawing me into an angle where we can't avoid being totally swamped."

"I shut all the doors," Jonathan offered, but she shook her head.

"You don't understand! It's not the water that's going to sink us. It's the sheer force of these huge waves crashing against the structure on top of the boat. It wasn't designed to take this!"

"Head into the waves directly."

"I'm trying! The boat's just not strong enough!"

Jonathan studied the controls and readouts, trying to find something that would help. One set of buttons read: "Turbo Boost."

Without asking Katherine first, he pushed both of them, and two orange lights came on. He couldn't feel anything, however. The storm was too rough to tell a difference.

He glanced out the window and caught his breath. The highest wave he had ever seen or imagined loomed in front of them like a skyscraper. He groped for something to hold onto.

"Katherine!" he yelled. "Do something!"

The wave loomed larger and larger until he couldn't even see the sky full of angry black clouds above them. Then, everything disappeared, and the boat lerched upward like a roller coaster car climb-ing the steepest hill. Jonathan closed his eyes.

When he opened them, they were still alive and intact. He glanced over at Katherine and noticed that her cheeks were dimpled. She was smiling.

"This isn't funny, Katherine!"

Another wave loomed on the horizon and she eased the wheel straight into it.

"We've got it!" she said. "Don't ask me how, but the boat's responding. We can handle this head-on."

Jonathan looked back at the orange lights on the console.

"We do make a good team," he said quietly, closing his eyes again as the boat thrust up with a gut-wrenching force.

"This is almost fun! We're going to make it,

Jon!"

Jonathan kept his eyes closed.

Chapter 8

AFTER TWO hours of tedious steering, and a major stomach ache for Jonathan, the effects of the storm began to diminish. Katherine even let Jonathan take a turn at the wheel with some of the smaller waves.

When the sun had returned and the waters steadied, they moved out onto the deck to inspect the damage. Behind the boat, the sky was black where the storm continued to rage.

"Look," Katherine said, "The dish is gone."

"Yes, how will Graham watch the Yankees?"

The both laughed, then Katherine wrinkled her nose and stared at him curiously.

"I never asked you—what did you do with them?"

"They're downstairs tied up."

He looked away, fully aware that she wanted to know more. He studied the aluminum roof of the great state room on the upper deck that had partially peeled back in one corner, and avoided her gaze.

"Okay, I give up. How did you do that?"

He relented and explained, finishing by saying

that, "the storm probably made the difference. Clarence came after me with a knife, but he couldn't keep his balance. So I knocked them out with a paper weight."

"That's original."

Jonathan nodded and looked around at the ocean which surrounded them like a dark blanket. Despite the fact that the sun was shining, the water remained black, the color of the storm clouds disappearing behind them. There was no sign of land in any direction.

"We'd better check the charts," Jonathan said. "The goons have to be using something to navigate with. We've got to be close by now, especially if the gale didn't blow us off course."

"Should we check on the twins?"

"No, they'll probably be out for a while."

THERE WERE no charts, but there were coordinates scrawled on a small piece of paper in Uncle Pinchbeck's cramped script. The note was taped to the console near the radio and small radar monitors.

"How do we check heading and bearing?"

"That's easy," Katherine said, pointing to one of the LCD displays. "That number, ninety-four, is our heading. The ship's instruments update that instantly and accurately, and they probably rigged this thing up to drive itself automatically to that heading."

"Is ninety-four the right heading?"

"That I don't know. We need a chart."

They both fanned out to search the pilothouse again for charts. There were empty drink cans and candy wrappers where the goons had left their mark, but little sign of deep navigational study.

"They couldn't have done this without charts!" Katherine said, annoyed, lifting up an empty metal tray with food crumbs all over it and looking underneath.

Jonathan thought about it for a moment. This island supposedly wasn't on the charts, so what good did the charts really do? In the middle of the Atlantic Ocean, there were no islands or landmarks to get your bearings on. Still, you needed some way to visualize the point in question, even if it was an invisible dot in the middle of the water on a map.

Uncle Pinchbeck was efficient. Everything he did was done the right way, or at least the efficient and profitable way. He would not have a million dollar ship unequipped with maps that could not get where it was supposed to go. He had been fanatical about Jonathan holding a map of a private school they once toured together, just in case they needed it. Uncle Pinchbeck's yacht had charts, somewhere.

"All the important papers were in his bedroom," Jonathan said after a moment. "That's where the map and letter were. Maybe we should check there."

"That doesn't make any sense, Jon. You steer the ship up here—not from the lowest, furthermost room under deck."

"Let's check anyway."

As they climbed down the stairs to the lower deck, the sun was making a strong appearance, washing the still-uneasy water in yellow heat. A strong salty, pungent odor filled the air, even below ship.

The goons were still unconscious. Katherine paused beside them, her face a mixture of anger and concern. "Are you sure you didn't kill them?"

"They're fine. And if it matters, they would've killed me."

They entered the bedroom, which was a wreck from the storm, Jonathan's fight with the goons, and was also the final resting place for many of their dirty clothes. Katherine looked at him, then herself in the mirror. They were barely fit to be called human. Their clothes were stained from salt water and sweat, which had now almost dried, leaving white blotches everywhere, and they were also torn and ripped in various places. Their faces were streaked, and their hair clumps of disheveled yarn.

"You look for the charts, Jon. I'll start a load of clothes."

He nodded and started searching. A moment later, he heard the hum of the washing machine, and then the shower.

Uncle Pinchbeck's desk was closed, so Jonathan carefully flipped it down and examined the contents. There were lots of papers and small booklets, but nothing that appeared to have anything to do with navigation. The letter and map, of course, were gone. Everything else appeared to be business papers.

One of them near the top said, "Belle Isle Case: Pinchbeck (formerly Osbourne) vs. The Republic of Martinkey." Mildly curious, since it seemed to be about an island, Jonathan opened it and read the first few lines aloud.

"Summary of case. Frank Pinchbeck, U. S. businessman and developer, laid claim to a small, uninhabited island about twenty miles off the northeast coast of Martinkey, based in part on the discovery of family papers that named him successor to the property. The Republic of Martinkey claimed ownership of the island, since it resides within the territorial sea limits of their outermost inhabited islands. During the trial, Pinchbeck failed to enter the family papers into evidence, claiming that privacy was an issue. The Republic of Martin-key failed to produce evidence that they had sur-veyed, or had any previous claim or knowledge of the island. The final decision of the Judge was abrogated when both parties reached an agreement outside of court which resulted in Pinchbeck pur-chasing the island from the Republic of Martinkey for an unspecified amount."

Jonathan quickly flipped through the minutes of the hearing, but it was more of the same. Then he noticed the date on the front page was over five years ago... five years!

The conversation he had overheard between his parents suddenly came back to him: "And don't ever let your brother see this! If he ever finds out about this..." And Jonathan had never been able to guess the remainder of what his father said. Now, perhaps he could. Somehow, Uncle Pinchbeck had found out about the island.

Many memories and thoughts came back to him; memories of Uncle Pinchbeck at picnics or other family events. He always avoided Jonathan's father, sliding away from his sister every time her husband came near. He always seemed to be thinking things that he wasn't saying.

He shuffled through more of the papers and found one that said, "Economic Development Blue-print for Belle Isle." He opened it and saw images of tall resorts and crystal blue waters. This was Treasure Island for Uncle Pinchbeck? Did he even care about the buried treasure from so many years ago, or the family tradition?

A voice behind him interrupted his thoughts. He spun around to see a welcome sight. Katherine was smiling, her dark blonde hair wet but combed; fresh shorts and t-shirt on. She looked like a teen-age girl again, and he could tell from the expression on her face that it was a great relief.

"You have some things clean in there, too," she said. Then, "Did you find the charts?"

She seemed to read the concern in his face, for she immediately came over and lifted the papers from him. She quickly glanced through them and then stared at him.

"Your Uncle has had this island for ten years?"

Jonathan nodded.

"He's building hotels on it?"

"I don't know. These are just plans. We don't really know what he's done with the island."

Katherine nodded, then said slowly, "What do you think your parents would have done if they found out when they got there that your Uncle had already beat them to the punch?"

Jonathan pressed his lips together for a second. "My father might have killed him."

Katherine shook her head. "Not really."

Jonathan shrugged. "How do we know my

parents didn't reach the island, then see something Uncle Pinchbeck didn't want them to see?"

Katherine's face turned serious. "You don't think your Uncle would hurt them, do you?"

Jonathan stared back at her. "I don't know."

Katherine repressed a shiver and pulled him away from the desk. "Come on, Jon. We've got to make sure we can get to the island before we worry about all of this. Your Uncle may be greedy, but I don't think he's some evil Mr. Hyde ready to trample on innocent people to get what he wants."

Jonathan wasn't so sure about that, but he withheld comment. Uncle Pinchbeck had provided for him materially, and tried to be a parent. But that still only bought so much trust.

They climbed the stairs slowly and returned to find the upper deck awash in sunshine, more brilliant than a few minutes before. Katherine squeezed his hand, and Jonathan turned with surprise to look at her, but she was staring at the horizon.

"Land!" she said, pointing with her other hand.

Chapter 9

SURE ENOUGH, Jonathan could see the faint out-line of an island in the distance. It was nothing more than a sliver of green on a dark blue table of ocean, but it was there. Toward the left side of it, a peak rose in the air that was clearly higher than the remainder of the island.

"The spyglass hill," Jonathan said slowly.

"The goons must have set the course in the ship for automatic pilot."

Jonathan nodded. "That might explain why they were so reluctant to take the helm during the storm—maybe they were afraid of messing up the coordinates, or something."

Katherine's face turned somber, her eyebrows crinkling. "We've got to get those two off the ship. If we leave them here while we explore, they'll find a way to get loose. We need to abandon them on the island, then move the ship to another shore."

Jonathan stared at her in surprise. The harshness in her voice was not characteristic. She returned his stare and seemed to understand what he was thinking.

"You said it yourself, Jonathan. They would have killed you. All we're doing is dropping them off until we can get help. We won't maroon them like Ben Gunn, forever."

Jonathan nodded slowly, still unsure about the idea.

On the horizon, the island began to loom larger. More details quickly showed themselves: pine trees, just as Stevenson had described them; flat, lengthy beaches, interspersed with jagged rocks and cliffs below the main promontory; a lazy cove that invited anchorage.

"This really is Treasure Island," he said.

Katherine nodded. "I didn't believe it until now, but I can smell it in the air. This really is where Long John's, or should I say Flint's, stash is. They never took the bar silver, remember?"

"Yes. Nor the jewels, or weaponry."

Katherine suddenly pushed them back into the cramped bridge and began studying the instruments again. Jonathan noticed that the digital compass still read "94."

"We've got to take over, now," Katherine said. "The autopilot won't park you exactly where you want to be. Ninety-four degrees can actually be hundreds of miles across when projected over a great distance, so I'm amazed that we just came up on it like this."

"My uncle would have to have it that way," he

reminded her. "Could the goons have done it them-selves?"

Katherine ignored him and began manipulating controls. The boat slowed down, and she gently steered it toward the cove. "We'll anchor there and take care of the goons first."

Jonathan nodded in agreement.

Then he thought about his parents and a surge of pain and excitement ran through him. This was their destination. If they were alive, this was where they would be. He stared at the approaching land form, but there was no sign of human activity.

He tried to rekindle that familiar feeling that always bounced around his head with so much certainty that he knew his parents were alive, but he found himself strangely empty. The island looked uninhabited.

Katherine's knowledge of seamanship was readily apparent as she maneuvered the boat into the calm waters of the cove. She even found the controls that released the anchor when they were several hundred feet from the wooded beachline.

Angry voices carried up to them from below. The goons were now awake.

"We'd better go ahead and deal with them," Katherine said, shutting down the engines.

Jonathan nodded, and happened to glance toward the shore as he exited from the navigator's cabin. He stopped suddenly when something in the corner of his eye appeared that wasn't expected. It was a person, standing on the beach beside a small dinghy waving an oar. There was, it seemed, civili-zation after all.

He tugged at Katherine's arm and pointed.

"Who is that?" she said, more annoyed than surprised. "I thought there weren't supposed to be any people on this island." She paused momentarily. "It's not your Dad, is it?"

Jonathan ran back into the cockpit and rummaged through the drawers until he found a set of mariner's glasses. He then jumped forward on the deck and focused them.

"Who is it?" Katherine said.

Jonathan twisted the knobs with a sinking feeling in the pit of his stomach.

"You're not going to believe this..."

"What?"

"It's Uncle Pinchbeck."

The figure on the beach stopped waving and climbed into the john boat.

"...And he's headed this way."

Chapter 10

JONATHAN COULDN'T explain why Uncle Pinchbeck's sudden, unexpected appearance didn't fit in with the rest of the idyllic picture. Hadn't they known he was going to be on the island at some point? After all, the goons were just meeting him there. They had all of his food and other supplies, if they weren't wrecked or lost during the storm.

The rowboat was half-way across the cove.

"What are we going to do, Jon?"

Between strokes with the oars, Uncle Pinchbeck was yelling unintelligible things at them. He was obviously not happy. This was undoubtedly not the kind of greeting he had expected.

"We can't let him get us. He'll probably lock us up like the goons."

"Your own uncle?"

"I don't think he wants us here. You saw those papers. I'm not sure we know everything about this island, or my uncle. He didn't want my parents here, either."

The dinghy was within hearing range. Uncle Pinchbeck's cramped, angry voice was clearly discernible.

"You were supposed to be in Savanna! I can't believe you're—"

Jonathan grabbed Katherine by the arm and led her to the stern of the yacht where Uncle Pinchbeck couldn't see them. Attached to the side of the boat was a small, sleek motorboat with room for two people—two fairly small people. The winch that lowered the boat was shiny and new, as if it had never been used.

Fortunately, it worked smoothly when Jonathan released the locking mechanism, and the boat was in the water only seconds later. Behind them, Uncle Pinchbeck was still ranting and raving as he pulled himself up the bow ladder.

"I hope this thing starts," Katherine said, jump-ing into the seat beside Jonathan, which actually required some wedging and twisting to fit securely.

Jonathan pushed the start button, and like all of Uncle Pinchbeck's toys, it started right up, purring like a big cat.

"Don't forget the line!"

Jonathan stretched to his side to release the guy wires, then gunned the engine. The boat started out in reverse.

"You're going backwards!"

Jonathan ignored her and searched for the gear pedal or switch. In the meantime, Uncle Pinchbeck arrived at the side of the boat.

"Young man, I am very disappointed in you! This is utterly beyond my comprehension! Do you know how much you upset Longfellow? Where are Clarence and Graham? Don't tell me they didn't come with you—I just talked to them by sat phone a day ago! Get up here and explain yourself."

"Sorry Uncle Frank," Jonathan said quietly, locating the lever and reversing it, then gunning the engine. "You have some explaining to do yourself!"

Uncle Pinchbeck's reply was drowned out in the roar of the engine. When they were a safe distance away, Jonathan slowed the engine and rode parallel to the bright white beach. They were both cramped and needed to get out and stretch soon.

"Do you think it's safe to land here?" Jonathan said.

Katherine looked behind them, where the yacht was a speck on the coast. Uncle Pinchbeck was nowhere to be seen.

"If we land, we'll need to move away from this part of the island, since he'll have the goons up before long and they'll be sure to search for us."

"If Uncle Pinchbeck was planning to develop Treasure Island, then he surely put some kind of facilities on it. Let's see what we can find. The island can't be that big."

"Five by ten miles," she said, "if I remember the book correctly. That's a lot of ground to cover."

"If it's like the original, then the best place for a shelter would be where the old stockade was, in the center below the spyglass hill."

He followed Katherine's glance across the terrain. The spyglass hill was not very far to their left, rising up like a mossy rock into the blue sky. Jonathan noted something curious on the hillside—something shiny, and metallic.

"Look at that, Kath. It's an antennae of some sort. A big one, too."

"Why would your uncle need that? Those are only used for satellite communications and long-range radio stuff."

"I don't know. Maybe it's got to do with phones. We had better get going, if we're going."

They clambered out of the small motorboat and tied it to a gnarled pine tree close to the water's edge. Uncle Pinchbeck would probably take it back into custody, but it was the best they could do under the circumstances.

Beyond the beach, the island was much wilder than it appeared from a distance. The foliage was jungle-like, with think undergrowth beneath tall canopied trees and bushes. There were hardwoods and pine trees that were typical of the western hemisphere in general, but also a number of unknown species that were the flavor of the tropics and climates further removed from North America.

Animal life flourished. Birds chirped and squawked everywhere, hidden in the dense greenery, sometimes flapping through leaves and branches when they passed too close. There were also squeals and screeches that sounded like monkeys.

"Monkeys?" Katherine said. "Surely not this far north of the equator."

"We're not that far north of it," he pointed out. "And we really don't know anything about this place. There could be predators here, too."

Katherine laughed tritely. "Now, I know that's not true. How would any tigers or gorillas or bears get here?"

Ahead of them, somewhere in the dense undergrowth of the jungle, a snarling animal hissed in reply. Katherine's face turned white and she drew up short on the more or less cleared path they were following.

Jonathan crouched and peered ahead. About twenty yards in front of them, a pair of glassy black eyes with yellow pupils stared at him through long, think ferns to the left of the trail. His heart skipped a beat when he gauged the distance from the eyes to the ground—it was a big black cat; probably a puma. It was obviously hunting. But something about its eyes wasn't right.

"Jonathan!" Katherine whispered. "Find a stick or something! We can't just sit here and wait for it to shred us up!"

"It's okay," he whispered back, looking to the right of the cat and nodding his head slightly. "Watch this."

As if on cue, the big cat lunged out of its hiding place and pounced on something to the right of the path.

"Look at the size of that snake!" Katherine said.

The constrictor tried to wrap itself around the neck of the black cat, but it wasn't fast enough. Claws and fangs tore at the snake's upper body with frightening efficiency, and in several second's time, the great reptile began to slow in it's move-ments. A minute later, it was perfectly still.

The cat looked up at them for a terrifying moment, then dragged the snake into the underbrush beside the path and disappeared.

"I guess there are some predators here," Katherine said slowly, her gaze traveling up and around them in all directions.

Jonathan pulled her forward along the path, carefully skirting around the area of the fight and the cat's hiding place. In the distance, the spyglass hill loomed larger, occasionally visible through the tree tops. The metallic glimmer of the antennae was more visible, too, a strange reminder that the island was not what it seemed.

What was Uncle Pinchbeck up to here? The birds and animals suddenly seemed to scream in a frenzied reply as he had the thought, and he slowed to check behind them for pursuit. There was no sign of activity, human or otherwise. Something about Treasure Island, however, definitely wasn't right.

Katherine drew her hair back into her hands and scanned the ground nearby, as if looking for something to tie it back with. Then she, too, stared ahead uneasily.

"This place is creepy, Jon. I have this weird feeling we're being watched, or something."

Jonathan nodded. "Do you still believe there's treasure here?"

"Yes, although maybe we should leave it be. I don't want the ghost of Flint or Long John Silver chasing me around, and there's definitely a lot of creepy things chasing around this place."

"I don't believe in ghosts."

And as the words came out of his mouth, they both saw straight in front of them the form of a eighteenth-century buccaneer appear, as if by magic, complete with saber and sash and a toothless scowl.

"What ye be wanting on this here isle?" he roared.

Jonathan was too shocked to respond.

Chapter 11

"WHAT ARE you staring at?" the pirate roared, drawing his saber and advancing. "Somebody cut your tongues out? Can't ya see that there's no trespassing on this here isle; nobody leaves alive, you see..."

Katherine took one step backwards and knocked Jonathan over. They both scrambled to their feet, still speechless.

"I can see you're a couple of little ones, yet, you are. But that's okay, because I was like you merself, once upon a time." The pirate replaced his saber and stroked his beard, as if contemplating what to do with the trespassers. "Yes, I was just like you."

He took two steps closer to them, and Jonathan could see beyond any shadow of a doubt that it was a real person; a real pirate. The hair on his chin was flecked with gray, and Jonathan noticed as well that his eyes were a piercing blue, and for some reason the pirate's haggard features didn't look totally unfamiliar.

Perhaps it was a picture in a book he had seen, Jonathan thought to himself.

"Who are you?" Katherine asked, her spunk returning quickly, at least on the surface. "If you're a real pirate, then you must have a name."

The pirate continued staring at Jonathan, even as Katherine spoke and he replied to her.

"Yes, mates, I do have a name, indeed."

Katherine's eyebrows arched. "Then what is it?"

The pirate smiled—a warm, totally unexpected gesture. He laughed once, then took his bandanna out of his haggard gray hair.

"The name's Lawrence Cox, yes it be!"

Yes, there was something familiar, indeed.

Jonathan rushed forward to embrace his father. They slapped each other on the back and laughed, and then his father's face darkened.

"We've got to get back to the shelter where your mother is. She's not well, and your uncle's men are not far away, and we've got a lot to talk about. He doesn't know that we survived the plane crash, but he's heard about the supposed ghosts of pirates." He winked at Jonathan and smiled at Katherine. "And who is this pretty young lady, Jonathan?"

Katherine introduced herself and shook Lawrence Cox's strong, friendly hand. "I've heard good things about you, Mr. Cox."

He nodded, then pushed them along the trail. "We really do need to move. How in the world did you avoid capture, or even get here for that matter? I came out here to scare your uncle's men, and they'll be coming after me with reinforcements in just a bit. They're starting to see through the hoax. Let's go, and then you can explain how in the world you managed to get to this forsaken place."

They hurried along the trail toward the spyglass hill. The path widened out gradually, and the trees began to thin and grow smaller. Another snake, much smaller this time, colored orange and yellow, scurried into the bushes, and Jonathan told his father of their recent encounter with the snake and wild cat.

Mr. Cox nodded his head. "Yes, I've seen one of those big cats, too. It doesn't make any sense—how could they possibly be native to these small islands?"

"Islands?" Jonathan said.

"Yes, this is just one of a number of small islands in the area. They all belong to some little country called Martinkey."

"Yes!" Katherine chimed in. "We read one of the papers that says Jon's Uncle owns this one, and went to court to prove it."

Mr. Cox pulled up short. "Really? Went to court? I can see that we have more to talk about than I even thought." He turned to Jonathan.

"Your Uncle is full of surprises."

Ahead, the path widened into a clearing at the base of the small mountain. In the center of the grassy area was a dilapidated structure that might once have been called a shack. Near a door hanging on one hinge, a pump went into the ground.

Mr. Cox pointed at it. "That's where we have to get our fresh water. Your Uncle's men get all of theirs further down the trail at a modern well near where they camp."

"You make it sound like he has an army here, or something," Katherine commented.

"In a way, he does. He's a real modern pirate."

"So this really is Treasure Island," Jonathan said slowly.

Mr. Cox waved around with his hand and smiled grimly. "Yes, it is, and your mother and I have had nothing but trouble since we found out about it. I guess money isn't everything."

Jonathan glanced at Katherine and they exchanged a look of confusion. His father was obviously disappointed—wasn't there any treasure left? he wondered. Or, had Uncle Pinchbeck stolen it all?

Katherine's expression looked particularly con-cerned.

Jonathan, however, found it hard to think about anything but his parents. They were alive, and he was reunited with them. Nothing else really matter-ed. It should have been a happy occasion.

"This way," Mr. Cox beckoned, leading them into the underbrush. "I've got to get back to your mother. She'll be delighted to see you."

HILLARY COX was, indeed, thrilled to see her son alive and well. Her physical appearance, however, stole away Jonathan's initial excitement. As she reached up from the grass mat she was resting on inside a crude hut hidden in thick underbrush, it was obvious from her weak arms and thin, drawn face that she was not well at all. Her eyes, however, still were alive, piercing green, like always.

"Jonathan! How on earth did you get here?"

Jonathan coaxed her to lay back down. "I hijacked Uncle Pinchbeck's boat."

Her face screwed up in a frown. "You've been staying with Frank?"

Mr. Cox laid a gentle hand on her shoulder reassuringly. "Hillary, it's my fault. We never revised the will, so he was the closest living relative, and he does have the money to take care of things like college and clothes."

She shook her head, her blonde hair dirty and matted. It was obvious she was sick if her hair looked like that.

"I don't care about the will, or college—I don't want our son staying with Frank! Not after all of this!"

Mr. Cox patted her on the shoulder and nodded. "I know, Hillary, I know. Jon is with us now, so let's not worry about it."

Mrs. Cox looked at Katherine, seemingly for the first time, and smiled deeply.

"This is my friend, Katherine," Jonathan said. "She's really smart, and she steered the ship herself during the storm."

Mrs. Cox smiled again and held Katherine's hand. "You're a very beautiful young lady," she said. "How on earth did Jonathan convince you to go on this kind of date?"

Katherine laughed. "Buried treasure."

Suddenly, both parents frowned and looked away.

"What did I say?" Katherine said quickly, look-ing at Jon.

"What is it?" Jonathan asked. "We saw the let-ter and the map. We know all about Robert Louis Stevenson being my great, great, great, great grand-father. We read Grandfather William's letter and we saw the map. We know about the treasure. It's still got to be here, unless Uncle Pinchbeck took it."

"Call him Uncle Frank!" his mother said, ob-viously trading what little strength she had for emphasis.

Mr. Cox, still bedecked as a pirate, sighed and sat down on the dirt floor of the hut. He tugged at his gray beard and looked at his wife. "I suppose we ought to start at the beginning. Why don't you rest, Hillary, and we'll go outside and talk."

She nodded slowly and turned over, trying to get comfortable on the thin mat.

Outside, Mr. Cox was still frowning. "She's been running a fever for two days now. I'm afraid it's some kind of tropical disease, and the aspirin ran out yesterday. We need something stronger, anyway."

"Why not get some from Uncle Pinchbeck's men?" Jon asked.

Mr. Cox stared at them emotionlessly for a long moment, almost as if he didn't understand the question. Then he finally said, "I think you'll understand after you hear this story."

Chapter 12

"AFTER YOUR mother found the papers in Grandfather William's attic, your Uncle Frank somehow got wind of it. He began pestering Hillary for the information, but she refused. It was difficult because your Uncle has always been involved in many shady business deals—like that time he changed his name from Osbourne to Pinch-beck, or the time he sold the land around Grand-father William's house without asking Hillary—and your mother and I decided that he would use the information for his own gain if we ever told him. Instead, we intended to explore it on our time and resources, then one day share it with you."

Mr. Cox smiled, almost whimsically, and stared into the jungle. "It was supposed to be an exciting little vacation for your mother and I; a romantic getaway. But then things began to go wrong. Just little things, at first, like our flight being changed to a smaller plane at the last minute, or the weather turning on us over the Atlantic, and then they even switched our landing field to a smaller island away from the capital city of Martinkey. None of this was suspicious at first.

"The storm got worse, however, and the pilot started to talk about turning back, or peeling off to the north. Of course he couldn't, because there wasn't enough gas. When things got really bad, he began to talk about crash landing on one of the smaller islands, or near enough to swim to one at least. I showed him the map of Treasure Island, and he tried to ditch us close to it.

"The storm was terrible. I really didn't believe we were going to make it. Somehow, the pilot got the plane down several hundred yards off shore, in the semi-protected area around the lagoon. We have a lot to owe him for, but he was injured during the crash. He didn't get out of the plane before it broke up, and we couldn't find him afterwards."

There was a moment or two of silence, and then he continued.

"Your mother and I made it to dry land, but everything in the plane was lost—including the map."

Jonathan suddenly reached down to feel his pocket—his own copy of the map was still there.

"Uncle Pinchbeck can do a lot of things," Katherine observed, "but he can't order a storm up any time he wants to."

Mr. Cox nodded. "That's true. But he could bribe the airline to give us a smaller plane, and divert our landing, to steer us further away from Treasure Island."

Jonathan thought about that for a moment. There were still some pieces of evidence missing. "I don't understand, Dad. There are no coordinates in the letter, or on the map. Yet we saw the coordinates pinned to the console—where did either of you get them? How did anyone know where to go?"

Mr. Cox grimaced and pulled uncomfortably at his beard. "I'm afraid that's my fault, too. The coordinates of the island were jotted on a third piece of paper that eventually was lost. At the time, I thought I misplaced it, but now I'm certain that we were burglarized by my own brother-in-law. Lucki-ly, I memorized the coordinates before that hap-pened."

Jonathan nodded, adding, "And we found papers on the *Victory* that say Uncle Pinchbeck bought this island from Martinkey years ago. He said that he had family papers to prove that he owned it, but he never produced them in court. He must have stolen them, copied them, then put them back in our house."

Mr. Cox looked grim. "I haven't figured that part out yet. The only thing I can say is that this whole rotten, disease-infested island stinks of your Uncle's plots."

"So there is no treasure," Katherine said quietly, looking very pained again.

Jonathan thought about her father—pitiful, often drunk, miserable man that he was, he was also her father, and no doubt devastated by her disappearance.

Mr. Cox's face lightened. "Actually, the treasure could still be here, I'm sure. Your uncle never believed that part of it, anyway. He just wanted the island itself."

Jonathan shook his head. "Now I'm really confused. Why wouldn't old moneybags want to get the treasure?"

"Come on," Mr. Cox said, standing up. "Let me show you what your uncle is really up to around here. Long John Silver would never have approved of it, I promise you."

Chapter13

THEIR JOURNEY through the forest took them to the eastern tip of the island, where sandy beaches formed a narrow border around the tall trees and dense undergrowth. They hadn't gone far, though, when they suddenly were confronted with a new obstacle—a shiny new, razor-sharp, barbed wire fence, with the lowest and highest strands electrified. Beyond it, and around a gentle curve, they could hear the muffled sounds of heavy equipment whining, but the rest of the view was cut off by trees and brush.

"What is he doing?" Katherine asked. "Building that resort we saw in the brochure?"

Mr. Cox's face rippled. "A resort? I don't think your Uncle is building a resort, contrary to what he might say to people."

"What is he doing, then?" Jonathan asked.

Jonathan's father walked over to the rim of the beach and held up a small amount of white sand in his palm. He brought it over for Jonathan and Katherine to study in the sunlight. When he turned his palm more directly toward the light, the fine grains of sand turned almost yellow.

"Rutile," Mr. Cox explained, "is an oxide mineral found in several parts of the world, including beaches in Georgia, near where your uncle lives. Most inland deposits, however, aren't pure. The deposits in sand are highly prized for their pureness and ease of extractability, but the majority of beaches where rutile is found are protected, and thus unavailable for industrial purposes."

"He's mining rutile," Jonathan said slowly, try-ing to think back through his many conversations with his Uncle to find a clue that might explain it. "Why?"

Mr. Cox shrugged. "I'm an accountant, remem-ber? I don't know everything, yet. I studied a little geology in college, but the only thing I know of that rutile is used for is making titanium. Unless your Uncle—"

"That's it!" Jonathan said, suddenly remember-ing. "Uncle Pinchbeck talked a lot about this com-pany in Connecticut that he was financing that was going to make nuclear submarines! He always looked at them on the stock quote's page!"

Mr. Cox nodded. "That would explain many things. These islands are protected by a weak, cor-rupt military government that would sell out for a pittance. Your Uncle wasn't interested in buried treasure—he wanted the rutile, cheap, illegal, and easy. In fact, he wanted it so badly that he almost got your mother and me killed, and we're not out of the fire yet."

Jonathan ignored the last part of what his father said and concentrated on the first part. "So the trea-sure is still here!"

Mr. Cox sighed. "We don't have the map."

Jonathan smiled and reached into his pocket.

"But we do, Dad. I made a copy of it back on the boat!"

A sound in the brush behind them interrupted their conversation. Mr. Cox pushed them down into the cover of vines and shrubs.

"Now you understand another thing about your Uncle," Mr. Cox whispered. "He's willing to kill people to preserve his secrets. I'm sure that's why those animals are here."

Jonathan nodded and exchanged a concerned glance with Katherine. Uncle Pinchbeck had imported the deadly animals, along with armed guards, barbed-wire fences, and who knew what else.

And to think that the island really should have belonged to his parents!

"It's just a goat," Mr. Cox said, pointing into the forest. "One of the few animals that really belong here naturally. Ben Gunn's cheese machines. Let's get back to check on your mother. If her fever doesn't break, all other plans won't matter."

Jonathan and Katherine nodded and followed him carefully back through the forest. Along the way, Mr. Cox suddenly seemed to remember what Jonathan had said a few minutes earlier.

"You have a copy of the map?"

"Yes. I took the precaution of making it because I didn't trust Uncle Pin—Uncle Frank."

"Well, the treasure may really be there, but right now it's the last thing on my priority list. The only thing I'm concerned about is all of us getting home safely."

Back at the crude campsite, Jonathan's mother proved to have taken a turn for the worse while they we were gone. She was feverish, and hardly seemed to recognize them. Her breathing came in short, wheezing gasps. She seemed to revive a little when Mr. Cox placed a wet rag on her forehead.

"You've got to go to Frank," she said quietly, closing her eyes again. "He's not totally inhuman."

Mr. Cox frowned. "He's already tried to kill us, Hillary. His men have been shooting at us! I can't just walk into his camp."

"Then you need to get the kids off the island. Forget about me, and just get them out safely!"

"You know that I can't leave you here."

She slipped back into a troubled doze and her grip on her husband's hand loosened. Mr. Cox sat down in silence beside her and stared into the ground.

Jonathan signaled to Katherine and they retreated to the edge of the camp, out of earshot.

"I'm going to Uncle Pinchbeck's camp," he said quietly.

"You can't do that, Jon, your dad won't let you. It's too dangerous."

"I don't have any choice, Kath. I came all this way because I knew they were alive, and now she might die if something isn't done. Dad won't leave her, and now he has to take care of us, too. I can't just sit here and do nothing."

"It's too risky, Jon. Wait and see what your dad wants to do."

"Risky? Compared to what—hijacking a ship and sailing through a mid-Atlantic gale?"

"Jon," she said sternly, "you know as well as I do that we hadn't counted on a lot of things, including your uncle's private army on this island."

"This island," he pointed out slowly, "is not just any island. This island is the Treasure Island. My Great Grandfather Stevenson immortalized this place. Imagine if people knew it really was here. Imagine the attention it would get. They would dig it up from one end to the other, and probably start charging admission."

"Don't forget that Uncle Pinchbeck would be getting all of the profits."

"Maybe not," Jonathan said, "and I don't think his purchase of the island will hold up in court if challenged back home. And that's not what's important, anyway. My parents came here for the treasure. We came here to find them, and also for the treasure. The treasure is still here. Uncle Pinch-beck supposedly hasn't bothered with the treasure yet, since he lost the map."

"But now that he knows we're here..."

"Exactly. We've got to get it before he does. He can set his army of thugs digging up everywhere. The island's not that big. They might get lucky."

Katherine squinted, as if she just at that moment understood the direction the conversation was taking.

"Jon, you can't get it alone. We've got to wait for your father. And your mother needs help! I want the treasure so bad I can see it even with my eyes open, but you've got to be realistic!"

Jonathan nodded, but in his mind he had already decided what he must do. He would sneak into Uncle Pinchbeck's camp, acquire medicine for his mother, dig up a good portion of the bar silver, and finally (and most importantly), steal some mode of transport for them all to get off the island. He was the most likely one to get past the guards, and he also might be the least likely to be shot if Uncle Pinchbeck were around—after all, Uncle Pinchbeck had been his parent for a while.

He would wait until the middle of the night, when everyone was asleep, and then he would slip away.

"You're not thinking of anything crazy, are you?" she asked him once more.

"No, of course not. You're right—I shouldn't go alone."

She looked at him suspiciously, but he said nothing else.

WHEN IT seemed that everyone was asleep, and the only sounds were of various tropical insects and tree frogs, Jonathan slowly raised his head from the floor of the crude shelter and looked around. Everyone was fast asleep.

Cautiously, and with painfully deliberate slowness, he pulled his father's jacket off, which had been serving as blanket, and put his shirt over his head. No one stirred.

Then, he crouched near the entrance to the forest and waited several minutes to make sure no one was about to wake. When they didn't, he moved off into the night, a little bit frightened, but a lot determined. Someone had to act. And wasn't he the one that had landed them in this mess? Hadn't it been his idea to stow away on his uncle's boat and go off in search of his parents and missing treasure? Things might have been simpler if he'd stayed in Georgia.

He paused along the trail, suddenly remembering the various creatures that inhabited the island. He was completely unarmed, carrying only the clothes on his back and the copied version of the treasure map. He would be easy prey for any creature—or man.

As if in reply to his thoughts, a low whistle emanated from the trees to his left, quieting the crickets and buzzing insects of the night. It sounded like a bird, or perhaps some small tree-climbing animal. Every spooky movie he had ever watched suddenly came back to him, including the one with real dinosaurs that softly whistled to each other when hunting their victims. Could Uncle Pinchbeck afford Velociraptors, as well as jaguars and pythons?

There was little hope in resisting, but he was not going to go down without a fight. He frantically beat around the brush until he found a dead piece of wood about the size of a baseball bat. Then, heart beating like crazy, he advanced in the direction of the whistle.

Something rustled in front of him.

With a low howl, he attacked blindly, thrashing the stick wildly in all directions. To his surprise, a voice rang out.

"Don't hit! It's me."

Katherine stood up slowly, brushing leaves and dirt from her clothing. "You could have really hurt me," she continued, moving out onto the trail be-side him. "You promised me you wouldn't do this by yourself."

Jonathan looked away sheepishly. He should have known that Katherine would find a way to tag along. Actually, he was relieved.

"I also thought you might need these."

She handed Jonathan a small lighter, and a hunting knife sheathed in a leather pouch. "I fi-gured your mom and dad wouldn't mind for a little while if we borrowed them for a good cause."

Jonathan flicked the lighter and pulled out the treasure map. How had he planned on studying the map in the dark?

He smiled at her, like old times. "Let's get to work, Kath."

"You're going for the silver before you get your mom medicine or find us a way off the island?" she said, worried.

Jonathan smiled. "Trust me. I've got a plan. The silver fits into it."

Chapter 14

THERE WERE no skeletons, or half-rotted corpses littering the path to the bar silver. Ben Gunn did not show up to lead the way. No pirates attacked them as they drew near. The ghost of Flint was silent.

The spot marked on the map was in the middle of a sandy ridge that overlooked Uncle Pinchbeck's rutile mining operation. Surprisingly, the cranes and heavy loaders were working nonstop through the night, their lights bright enough to illuminate the waves crashing near by.

"Is that ritalyn stuff really worth that much?" Katherine asked.

"I don't know. You don't think they'll see us up here, do you?"

Katherine turned in a slow circle, examining the terrain all around them. There was no sign that anyone had been in this particular spot since Flint and his six unfortunate crewmen had buried the heavy bars of silver ingot hundreds of years ago.

She shook her head. "They might during the day, but not at night."

"Good. Let's get to work."

Katherine smirked. "Okay, Jon. What are we going to dig with?"

Jonathan leaned over and pushed the dirt with his hands—the loose, sandy soil flaked away easily.

"But, Jon, it could be anywhere within twenty of feet of where you're standing, and it could be ten feet deep!"

He pulled the map out and pointed to one of the cryptic marks they had puzzled over. "Do you see this tree? It's still there, if I'm right—that one right there. The map shows it lining up directly with the spyglass hill."

"That can't possibly be the same tree, can it?"

"It's some kind of hemlock. They can live for hundreds of years, I think."

Katherine remained skeptical. Jonathan chose to continue digging while she went over to the gnarled trunk of the cedar and examined it closely. The dirt pulled away easily, and the new problem developing was where to put the material he displaced. The pile he had already made was sliding back into his hole.

He paused when he heard Katherine make a strange sound. At first, he thought she had found something on the tree, but then he could tell that she was looking beyond it.

"Someone's coming, Jon!"

Before panic could set in, Jonathan studied the

ground calmly and made a decision. Not that much dirt had been displaced. He simply filled his hole back in and smoothed the sand to make it appear as natural as possible. The chances were slim that anyone would notice.

Katherine grabbed him by the shoulder and dragged him into the bushes on a small rise across from the clearing.

Moments later, a light appeared in the darkness, bobbing around as if disembodied. As it drew clo-ser, Jonathan could see a human shadow carrying it. Voices also became audible.

"But Mr. Pinchbeck, we checked the wreckage. No one could have survived that crash." Graham's voice was unmistakable.

"What about bodies, or pieces of bodies? I told you not to come back without evidence!" Uncle Pinchbeck was still dressed in a tie and slacks, of all things, as if just leaving an important business meeting.

Clarence snarled at Graham, who closed his mouth and let his partner speak. "It's like he said, Mr. Pinchbeck, no one could have lived in that plane if the crash caused the damage. Besides, we found the pilot's body. How could they have lived, if he didn't make it? I suppose he might have landed safely, then abandoned the plane. Maybe the waves could have washed it on the rocks. But why was his body on the beach, then, and not their's as well? There's no sign of them anywhere. My edu-cated guess is that they're dead, sunk to the bottom of the sea somewhere."

"I can guess, too, you fools!" Uncle Pinchbeck snarled. "I pay you to find hard evidence, or to per-form manual labor, if you will. Leave the guessing to me! If they survived, and check the airport transcripts at Martinkey, they'll—"

Suddenly, the three of them drew up short at the sandy clearing, and Clarence focused the flash-light on a paper in Uncle Pinchbeck's grasp. The map! Uncle Pinchbeck, as expected, still had his copy.

"This is it," Clarence said triumphantly. "Bar silver, huh?"

"And weapons, too," Jonathan whispered to himself.

Uncle Pinchbeck ignored Clarence, who started trying to talk about the missing bodies again, and suddenly moved over to the area where Jonathan had been digging, hovering suspiciously over the ground.

"Someone's been digging here..."

Clarence frowned in mid-sentence, then smiled. "Maybe it was Ben Gunn!" he said, laughing ridi-culously at his own joke.

"Who's Ben Gunn?" Graham said, a look of confusion all over his face.

"Shut up!" Uncle Pinchbeck ordered. "Both of you! They beat us to the punch. Look right here—" He pointed at the sand. "They tried to cover it up, but they were here all right."

Both of the goons leaned over and stared.

"You mean your nephew and that friend of his?"

Uncle Pinchbeck stared at them for a long time, as if exasperated. "No, I mean the dead pilot came up here and did it, you idiots!"

Clarence and Graham looked each other, then stayed clamed up for the moment.

Katherine tugged at Jonathan's sleeve.

"What now, genius? We need a new plan."

He frowned, but said nothing. Another crazy idea was beginning to form in his head. It was a plan so crazy, that it just might work. Most of his other crazy plans had worked. It would require Katherine's cooperation, though, and a little bit of good luck. The main thing he was counting on was Uncle Pinchbeck acting like—well, like Uncle Pinchbeck. That was a fairly sure thing wasn't it?

"Katherine," he whispered, "I want you to promise me that you'll take the medicine to my mother."

"What do you mean?"

"Just promise."

"Okay."

"After they take me, follow behind us at a safe distance."

"What?" she said, straightening up.

But Jonathan was already moving out into the clearing. Graham heard him first, and pulled a gun from his jacket, which he aimed straight at Jonathan.

"Put your hands up!"

Uncle Pinchbeck and Clarence turned around.

"I think we need to talk," Jonathan said, trying to project confidence into his voice. "I have something you want, and you have something I want."

"Well, well," Uncle Pinchbeck chortled, drawing nearer, "if it isn't my nephew Jonathan, alive and well. Shiver me timbers!"

Graham continued to hold the gun leveled at him.

"I've got the silver," Jon lied.

Uncle Pinchbeck's expression soured and he glanced over his shoulder at the marks in the sand. "You do, do you? Let me guess—you stowed it in Ben Gunn's cave."

Graham, and especially Clarence, started guffawing, but Uncle Pinchbeck's face remained totally cool, as if trying to read Jonathan's mind.

"As a matter of fact, I do have it there." Jonathan kept his face serious. "It's the one place I know of that you don't have marked on your map."

Graham and Clarence stopped laughing.

Uncle Pinchbeck loosened his red tie, then shrugged. “So you have the silver. I can find it. My men can find anything on this island.”

Jonathan almost opened his mouth to argue that point, then caught himself. It was more useful if Uncle Pinchbeck thought Jon’s parents really were dead.

“I came here to find my parents,” Jonathan continued, but much more carefully now.

“Your parents? Why would they be here?”

“You know why. Their little Atlantic getaway? She’s the one who found the map! You can act like I’m crazy, but I figured out that they were coming here on their vacation. I heard you talking about their bodies!”

Uncle Pinchbeck shrugged innocently. “Some workers drowned. I don’t know how that relates to your parent’s disappearance.”

“I also wanted the treasure, since I discovered that it really should have been my mother’s.”

His uncle’s face flashed. “It may interest you to know, coincidentally, that male heirs usually take precedence. And as for your parents, I’ll search the island for them, but I’m sure they would have shown up by now if they were alive, and it really is crazy to think they were coming here!”

“You forget, Uncle Frank—”

"—Pinchbeck!"

"You forget that I know all about the letter. My mother found it. You had to steal it from her."

"That's preposterous, Jonathan! I would never steal anything from Hillary!"

Graham began to fidget. Jonathan stared straight at both of the goons. "Maybe you didn't. You could always afford to have someone else steal it for you."

Uncle Pinchbeck laughed nervously.

"You're growing up too fast, Jon." His face suddenly softened. "And you must be very tired. And where is that pretty little friend of yours? We all can go get something to eat and talk about this."

Jonathan shook his head. "No. She's guarding the silver." In the back of his mind, he realized that his uncle was cleverly steering the conversation away from his parents. Actually, though, that could work in Jonathan's favor.

"Then you, Jon, come on with me to the barracks and let's get something cool to drink and have a big snack. I'm sure you haven't been eating well. Then we'll sort this whole mess out." Uncle Pinchbeck tried to lighten things up by laughing, but he ended up sounding completely insincere. "Then we'll get you on a plane out of here."

"There's an airstrip here?"

"Of course—why do you ask?"

"Actually," Jonathan said slowly, wiping his forehead, "I think I'm coming down with something. I could use some aspirin and some kind of antibiotic..."

"Fine, fine, there's a medical station in the barracks. Let's go." Uncle Pinchbeck started to walk away, then pointed back at the sand and the goons. "You two stay here and start digging."

"Yes, sir," came the tandem reply.

"The treasure's not there. What's the matter," Jon said quickly, "don't you believe me?"

Uncle Pinchbeck smiled, and a funny feeling passed through Jonathan's stomach. "Of course I believe you, nephew. But they need the exercise. It certainly can't hurt them."

"I hope the animals get them," Jonathan mutter-ed, moving towards the trail behind Uncle Pinch-beck. "Or, Flint's ghost! I should have warned you that we dug during the day, because Flint comes out at night."

"Who's Flint?" Graham said to Clarence, setting his lantern down and picking up a shovel. "Did he say ghost?"

Jonathan turned the corner on the trail and didn't hear the reply. He could imagine what Clarence was saying to his less intelligent, easily persuaded co-worker.

In the meantime, the silence between him and

his uncle lasted so long that eventually he felt like he had to make conversation.

"I thought you might kill me when I saw you coming to the boat," Jonathan said, laughing nervously.

"I just might, yet," came the icy reply. The silence resumed, and if anything, Uncle Pinchbeck picked up his already frantic pace. It was the way he always walked when in the midst of an important business deal.

"So much for conversation," Jonathan said to himself.

He only hoped that Katherine had heard his hidden clues. She was smart; she would know what to do. The goons were no match for her. Flint's ghost would appear, yet, and if he knew Katherine, it would be show-stopper.

Chapter 15

THE "BARRACKS" was in reality a complex of new buildings that centered around a small lagoon near the mining operation. Uncle Pinchbeck had obviously invested a lot of time and money in the Treasure Island. There were Landrovers, ATVs, and Jetskis, even the *Victory* at quiet dock, along with a freighter that must have been for the rutile. The atmosphere was that of a small militarized resort, if such a thing could be possible.

The path widened considerably near the complex, and an armed guard manned a checkpoint. He barely nodded at Uncle Pinchbeck as they walked by.

"Why all the security?" Jonathan asked.

"There are lots of sharks around," his uncle replied. "You could even call them pirates, if you want to use that term. That buried treasure has nothing to do with why I need this island."

"It's illegal to mine rutile from beaches."

Uncle Pinchbeck smirked and shook his head. "Not in Martinkey. And besides, rutile isn't the only valuable thing here. This will be the biggest historical resort ever built when I'm done with the place."

Jonathan nodded. So Uncle Pinchbeck was going to build the resort. "But if you stole the map from my mother, then—"

"Shut up!" Uncle Pinchbeck said loudly. "That's always been your problem—you think you know everything! Just like your father. If I had any sense about me, I'd throw you in the brig!"

"You have a brig here?"

"Of course I do. I have everything here."

He led Jonathan into the lobby of a building where an army of snack and drink machines lined the wall. He motioned for Jonathan to sit down and began feeding money into the machines. A minute later, there were chips, cookies, crackers, and pop-corn, along with two sodas and some chewing gum.

"Eat up, Jonnie."

What happened to "eat all your peas?" Jonathan wondered. He began munching some chips, then pressed forward with things.

"I really have some kind of flu, Uncle. Can you get me some kind of antibiotic?"

Uncle Pinchbeck sighed. "I suppose so. The infirmary is right around the corner. You just sit here, okay?"

"All right."

Uncle Pinchbeck jumped up and muttered over his shoulder, "It should be painfully obvious why I never had any children of my own."

"It is painfully obvious," Jonathan said under his breath.

While Uncle Pinchbeck was busy around the corner, Jonathan leaped up to the plate glass windows and studied the complex. Any one of the big speed boats swaying at anchor would be big enough to get them to Martinkey, and then the outside world. He would need a key. Then he would steer the boat to the lagoon where the *Victory* had originally anchored and pick everyone up.

They would also need evidence when they reached the outside. Jonathan and Katherine had both heard him confess to several crimes, but who would believe two kids? Before they left, Jonathan would have to snare some hard evidence. The airport might be the place.

"I thought you were hungry?"

"I am!" Jonathan said scrambling back to his seat and jamming food into his mouth.

"Well, here's some stuff the doc said will take care of your jungle fever, although I must confess you look okay to me."

"The food is having its effect." Jonathan shoved the medicine in his pocket. "I'll take this later, if I start feeling worse again."

Uncle Pinchbeck pulled a metal chair out across from Jonathan and sat down with a thump.

"It's time for you and me to start talking."

Jonathan swallowed some more chips and stared at Uncle Pinchbeck. In some ways, he really was not an evil or terrible person. At certain moments, he actually gave the appearance of a normal human being who harbored real feelings and sympathy for his fellow man.

"Jonathan," he said quietly. "I've been thinking about your parents—about Hillary. Maybe I was wrong. If they were trying to come here, as you say they were, then I need to have the island searched again. There are many isolated little coves and val-leys where they might be waiting for help. Would you like to take one of the ATVs tomorrow with some of my men and do that?"

Jonathan stared really hard now. Was he being serious? "Yes," he said slowly. "Of course I'll do that."

"Good. If they're alive, we'll find them." He slapped Jonathan on the knee. "I still don't understand, however, what makes you think your parents had more claim here than me. We found the map at the same time, and I had the fortune to exploit it first. Your mother, now that I've thought about it, is entitled to half of everything here. But consider, too, that it was my money that bought the island. She'll have to reimburse me for that."

"Okay," Jonathan said, shaking his head dizzily. Had his uncle gone totally crazy? He was going to split the money; expected reimbursement for his crimes?

"There's also the little matter of the silver you've hidden."

"Right," Jonathan said quickly. "When things settle out, you'll get your half."

Uncle Pinchbeck slapped him on the knee again.

"Let's shake on this nephew—no hard feelings!"

Jonathan shook Uncle Pinchbeck's hand limply and studied his pock-marked, smiling face. Was he being sincere?

"You'll forget about me stealing your boat for a few days?"

"Of course!" Uncle Pinchbeck said.

"And you'll give my mother half the treasure?"

"If she's still alive. If not, it will go to you."

"And the private school in Savanna?"

Uncle Pinchbeck stroked his chin for a moment. "We'll have to discuss that when we get back."

Jonathan stood and pushed all of the wrappers and crumbs away on the table. "You're really serious about this, Uncle Pinchbeck?"

"Totally serious."

Jonathan nodded. "Okay."

"Okay! Come on and I'll show you where you can bunk. Tomorrow we'll start searching at the crack of dawn."

JONATHAN DIDN'T stay long in the sparse room he was dropped off at. Instead, after watching Uncle Pinchbeck leave the building and enter another one down the street, he decided it was time to do some sleuthing.

There were no guards in this particular building, which was like a small dormitory, and no one saw Jon slip into the night and trace the steps of Uncle Pinchbeck to a square-shaped, brightly lit glass building in the center of the complex. There were armed guards at the entrance to this building.

Funny, Jonathan thought again, that Uncle Pinchbeck would need all of this security for a legal operation.

The guards were sitting at a counter filled with monitors, behind a set of double doors. Between the outer and inner doors were small alcoves, where strange modernistic sculptures that looked like pieces of scrap metal from fifty years ago sat dumbly. If he were in one of the alcoves, the guards wouldn't see him.

He watched them for a long time, and after a while he noticed that they would laugh, or roll around in their chairs, which totally blocked their vision of the doors. The third time they did this,

Jonathan silently slipped through the first set of doors into the left alcove. Once there, he cautiously peered around the corner to study their actions again.

They were clearly bored and looking for a little excitement. Jonathan fumbled in his pockets and found the lighter Katherine had borrowed from his parents. He also had the hunting knife. A plan was hatched.

From his other pocket he pulled two candy bars that Uncle Pinchbeck had shoved into his hands on the way out of the vending area. He unwrapped them and shoved the bars into the middle of the nearest sculpture. Actually, he thought it made the monstrosity look better. Then he set the wrappers on the floor and lit them with the lighter.

Quickly, he dashed across to the opposite alcove, then wheeled and threw the hunting knife as hard as he could at the glass windows in the opposite alcove. The glass didn't shatter, but it did crack with a loud bang, and the guards were instantly stumbling over themselves to find out what it was. Jonathan pushed himself behind a half-pillar of marble as they flew out.

Of course they saw the window, but they also saw the small fire, which was threatening to catch the plush orange carpet on fire.

"Put that out!" one of them yelled at the other.

Jonathan had already slipped right behind them into the lobby, and then past the counter. He turned the corner, and undetected, made it to the elevator.

Inside the elevator, there were four choices. Level four said, "COMMAND." Apparently, Uncle Pinchbeck felt secure enough not to bother hiding that.

When the elevator opened to the fourth floor, Jonathan's eyes grew wide. Uncle Pinchbeck was standing right in front of him, with a phone jammed to his ear, his back turned to the elevator and hallway. Jonathan quickly ducked down behind an unoccupied desk that the secretary probably used during business hours.

Surprisingly, he was close enough to hear the conversation.

"That's right," Uncle Pinchbeck said. "I agree with you, Bill. But first I've got to take care of this thing with my nephew."

Jonathan nearly bumped his head under the desk.

"Well, you have kids, so I'm sure you understand. But the real problem is that he's too smart. He's figured too many things out. In fact, if I let him hang around here very long, he'll know everything."

Jonathan's stomach was growing very tight.

What more was there to know?

"Well, for starters, he's suspicious about the plane wreck. You need to get over to Martinkey for me and discreetly change the flight records. I don't care how much it costs.

"Then, I need you to bring those dogs over so we can cover every square inch of this island. He thinks Hillary is still alive, and I'm not going to take any chances."

Jonathan clinched his fist, and then suppressed a scream. Uncle Pinchbeck was going to kill his parents if he found them!

"That's the problem, Billy boy. If this thing ever goes to court, Hillary is the one person who can punch legal holes in my ownership of the island."

Jonathan's mind started whirling one-hundred miles an hour. He had to get the medicine back to his mother, but he also had to get them off the island. Maybe even tonight.

"And by the way," Uncle Pinchbeck said as he was winding up, "some of the men have been acting spooked. Did you put some new kind of critter out there that you didn't tell me about?"

There was silence for a moment.

"You're as crazy as they are, Bill! Flint's ghost is no more real than the treasure, although I've got Clarence and Graham out there with the map looking for it." Uncle Pinchbeck laughed uproariously, as if that was more than funny, and Jonathan almost felt sorry for the goons for a moment. It passed quickly, though. After all, they had tried to kill him.

As Uncle Pinchbeck finished hanging the phone up, Jonathan dashed back onto the elevator, then sailed right past the security guards before they knew what happened. He briefly heard them screaming and yelling just before the sound-proof doors closed.

Chapter 16

THE BIG boats were his first target—perhaps even the *Victory* itself. With one of them, he could circle around the island quickly and actually gain time re-turning to the shack and his parents, not to mention the benefit of using it to completely leave the island.

He didn't reach the big boats, though, before a siren suddenly wailed and lights flashed on every-where. Armed men scurried about like ants. Reach-ing the big boats was now out of the question.

There were, however, Jetskis parked at nearby quays. Jonathan hopped on the closest one, a brand new bright pink and lime green model, and reached down for the key. Fortunately, whoever was in charge of all the equipment around the base didn't feel it was necessary to keep the keys locked up. The Jetski started immediately.

He happened to look back in the direction of the main building and saw with a start that Uncle Pinchbeck had joined the fray, shouting directions and looking around wildly for his wayward neph-ew. As Jonathan eased the Jetski out of its slip,

Uncle Pinchbeck somehow spotted him in the confusion. Twenty armed men converged on the dock area.

Jonathan didn't stop to watch them. He gunned the Jetski and headed into the darkness of the lagoon. He knew that if he should he happen upon a hidden sandbar or submerged log, he was as good as dead. Beside him, the water began to sparkle—the guards behind him were shining their flash-lights around like spotlights.

"I want to go east," he said to himself, trying hard to focus only on what he could control—not things completely beyond it. "That would mean turning right after the spit that goes out into the ocean beyond the lagoon. That means the lights from the cranes should be visible."

He strained his eyes in the darkness, but there was no sign of the gigantic rutile-mining machines that worked down the beach a short distance away. He couldn't see the finger of sand, either. How far out did the spit go? Was he beyond it already?

He veered to the right and the Jetski abruptly whined in protest and shivered violently. He swerved back to the left. He was right next to the spit, probably in less than a foot of water.

To make matters worse, the water began to erupt around him. Uncle Pinchbeck's men were actually shooting at him!

He turned around and found to his dismay that

three of the guards were almost upon him. Whatever machines they were riding on were evidently faster or more powerful than his own Jetski. They gestured with their guns that he should pull over.

Instead, acting on a sudden impulse, he whipped the Jetski directly right at a ninety degree angle and held on for dear life. The machine hit some-thing hard then vaulted into the air for what seemed like an eternity. A second later, it crashed into the surf and he swallowed a mouthful of salty water before it popped back to the surface. Spluttering and coughing, he looked back and saw that his pursuers were attempting to do the same thing.

The first driver ran aground and was completely stuck. The second struck something hard and the driver jumped off just as his machine exploded in a fiery blast. The third driver thought better of it all and continued to the end of the spit to swing around and maintain the chase.

But now their lights had lost him. Jonathan gunned the engine and opened it up as wide as the throttle would go. With any luck, he could be back in the shack within an hour or so. He reached down and patted his pocket—the medicine was still there.

Then his stomach sank. What about Katherine? He had forgotten the predicament he left her in. He would have to go there first on the way to his parents. What if the goons had overpowered her? He pushed the thought out of his head. Escape was first.

When the lights of the cranes finally loomed near, he slowed down and looked for a good hiding place along the beach. The Jetski might yet come in handy. A few minutes later, he cautiously ap-proached the sandy plateau where the treasure presumably lay buried.

All seemed quiet at first. As he ventured out of the trees, however, he detected a low noise like someone moaning. Concerned, he bolted across the clearing and nearly tripped over the prostrate forms of Graham and Clarence. They were both marginal-ly conscious, each leaning back against the other with hands firmly tied.

A sound in the brush behind him caused him to wheel around defensively, only to discover a smiling, triumphant Katherine.

"How did you do that?" he said in awe.

"I hit them over the head with a bar of silver."

Jonathan stared at her. It took a moment for the information to sink in. Then, he straightened up with a clenched fist and shouted. "Yes! Where is it?"

Katherine shook her head. "That can wait. Aren't you forgetting about something?"

Jonathan stared at her blankly, then reached

down to his pocket. The medicine was still there.

"Let's get that to your mom now."

Jonathan nodded and turned toward the trail. As they passed the goons, he wondered out loud, "do you think the ghost of Flint will get them?"

"He already did," Katherine replied, but more than this she wouldn't tell him.

THE MEDICINE seemed to take effect on Jonathan's mother right away. A few minutes later, she was sitting, sipping water and inquiring about what snacks they might have lying around.

Mr. Cox pulled Jonathan and Katherine outside again for another hushed consultation.

"What did you find out?"

"Uncle Pinchbeck's planning on searching the entire island with dogs," Jonathan said. "I think we should leave tonight."

His father's eyebrows went up a notch. "I agree. Your mother, even though improved, still needs some serious medical attention. To leave, however, will require a boat. We'll probably have to sneak into the main compound to get one."

Jonathan bit his lip and smiled sheepishly. "I don't think that's such a good idea."

"Why not?"

Jonathan told him about the trip to the bar silver, and the run-in with the goons and Uncle

Pinchbeck; and then about the trip to the compound, the medicine, and the Jetskis.

"You two have been pretty busy tonight," Mr. Cox said.

Jonathan also told him about the phone conversation he had overheard. Mr. Cox shook his head sadly, then responded angrily.

"Your uncle is a terrible person! He's always been smart and talented—just like Hillary—but he's twisted. When we get back, he's going to find that he'll need a very good lawyer to get out of this one. It won't be something simple like the name change. But until we leave the island, there's no telling what lengths he'll go to to stop us. We need to leave tonight, and we need to get those records from the airport before he does."

"I have a Jetski," Jonathan offered. "We also have lots of silver."

"We may have to come back later for the silver," Mr. Cox said.

Katherine cleared her throat, and Jonathan sensed that she was either protesting about the treasure, or trying to share one of her creative ideas that she always seemed to come up with.

"I think we should steal back the *Victory*," she said. "It's not only the safest and newest ship in harbor, but it also has the evidence you want—all of those papers about the court case and the development of the island as a resort."

"That's great," said Jonathan, "but the *Victory* is parked in the middle of the complex, and after my little adventure, that area will be swarming with guards."

Mr. Cox stroked his chin. "It seems to me like what we need is a diversion; something exciting enough to draw them away from the *Victory* so one of us can get aboard and sail it out of the lagoon unnoticed. What would be the most important thing to protect on the island, as far as your uncle is concerned?"

"The treasure?" Katherine said, her voice unsure.

"No!" Jonathan countered. "The rutile operation! That's what he said was making them so much money!"

"Exactly," Mr. Cox said. "If we sabotage one of those big cranes, and we're loud enough about the whole thing, those guards will leave the compound, and the boats will be more vulnerable."

Mr. Cox returned to check on Jonathan's mother. Katherine sat down beside Jonathan and sighed.

"Do you really think this will work?"

"Of course," he answered.

"Do you think we'll get the treasure, or is it bad for me to even worry about that?"

Jonathan grabbed her hand and held it. "I

realize its not the money you're really after," he said quietly. "We won't leave without the treasure."

She smiled at him, and Jonathan completely understood what she was really talking about. The treasure symbolized the conquest she was attempting in her own personal life. It had little to do with money, and a lot to do with psychology. It had to do with overcoming obstacles: poverty, loss of a mother, and a father more concerned with a bottle than the future.

"Let's get to work," Mr. Cox said cheerily, returning. "We've got some havoc to wreak."

Katherine smiled when Jonathan winked at her.

JONATHAN AND Katherine hunched down fifty feet away from the guard post where he had originally entered the compound. At the small booth located there, six armed men were milling about, unsorting a tangle of barking German Shepherds.

"I didn't know German Shepherds were trackers," Katherine whispered.

Jonathan shook his head. "This is really bad. If those dogs get loose now, they'll find mom before we or dad can get back to her. We've got to stop them."

Katherine buttoned the sweater up that Jonathan's mother had loaned her against the chill of the late night air, then pointed toward the distant lights on the cranes. "Your dad is about to do his part. We've got the get the boat. If we get it, we can beat the guards to your mom."

"That's cutting it too close!"

Before Katherine could respond, a muffled whump sounded from the direction of the nearest crane. At first, nothing else happened. Then the lights blinked off, and without warning, a terrible explosion rocked the whole island.

"Wow," Katherine said, in awe, "how did he do that?"

Jonathan didn't answer her. He was studying the guards. One of them was talking on the phone in the booth. Seconds later, all six and the snarling, snapping herd of dogs were headed down the trail to the first crane. They passed with a few yards of Jonathan's hiding place talking in low, excited, somewhat angry voices.

"Come on!" Katherine said. "We've got to go get the boat!"

She pulled Jonathan out of the brush and they entered the compound, cautiously staying close to walls, trees, or any other natural cover. Other guards were around, jumping into ATVs or running in and out of buildings, but none of them seemed to be on the lookout for two teenage saboteurs.

"We'd better hope the key is in it," Katherine said.

"It will be. Uncle Pinchbeck always assumes too much. The Jetskis all had keys, too."

"Over there it is," she said, pointing. "We'll have to make a dash across the square."

They waited until it seemed like no one was around, then ran across the road to the docks where the *Victory* and several other boats were moored. Incredibly, repairs had already been done on much of the storm damage. They quickly climbed aboard and checked the pilothouse door. It was unlocked.

"With any luck, they'll think it's my uncle taking the boat out and won't even question it."

"This should start it up," Katherine said, turning a gold key and pushing a red button. Beneath them, the floor shook slightly and a faint purr could be heard.

"Untie us, Jon. I'll figure out how to back out."

Jonathan scrambled outside and started untying the rope that secured the *Victory* to the dock. After several unsuccessful attempts, he realized with embarrassment that the rope was simply looped and could be lifted off the hook, and was not meant to be untied. Fortunately, Katherine hadn't noticed.

"Go!" he said.

The boat eased backwards into the blackness of the lagoon, then started forward. Katherine was a good pilot. Jonathan rejoined her in the pilothouse as she headed the *Victory* out toward the spit. So far, no alarm had been raised.

"We'll have to anchor beyond the cranes, near where the treasure is," he said. "The alarm will get out quickly, so we'll have to move fast. Once we get to Martinkey, we can call the police."

Katherine nodded and slowed the throttle as the boat neared the end of the spit. "Why don't you go look for those papers you found downstairs? We'll need those when we get the police, won't we?"

"Good idea."

Jonathan started downstairs. At the bottom, he flipped the light switch and nothing happened. Strange. The repair crew must not have fixed that yet.

He fumbled his way through the dark to the bedroom desk and rummaged through the contents. His stomach sank as he realized that they were no longer there.

"Looking for something?" a low voice said in the dark.

Jonathan nearly jumped out of his skin. He turned around and saw the glint of a gun barrel illu-minated by a flashlight, as well as the horrible, shadowy face of his uncle. Uncle Pinchbeck smiled.

"I should have known that I couldn't trust you," he said slowly, inching closer to Jonathan. "But in matters of family, I've always erred on the for-giving side. Would you mind telling me exactly where you plan on taking us tonight?"

Jonathan backed up a step and found himself against the wall. There was nowhere else to go. "Just a little joy ride. Maybe pick up a little trea-sure..."

Uncle Pinchbeck laughed loudly. "Treasure? Is that why you needed the medicine? Please, give me a little credit, Jonnie. At least one of your parents is alive, and all of those 'ghosts' my men have been seeing were undoubtedly your father's creation. It's quite unfortunate that Hillary took that letter from Grandfather William so seriously. I should never have returned it after I stole it and photocopied it."

"You're admitting to that?"

Uncle Pinchbeck smiled again. "I have no secrets now. In just a little while, I'm afraid a ter-rible accident will happen. A vacationing family will drown in an usually rough surf. The bodies will be discovered by a caring relative, who will return them to the states for burial..."

"You'd kill your own sister and nephew?"

"Of course not!" he said quickly. "It's a terrible accident we're talking about. After enough time has passed by, all of the legal details regarding this island will be pushed through quietly without any protest. Then, this new Treasure Island story will be complete!"

"You're evil! You won't find my parents. I won't take you to them!" Jonathan started to run up the stairs to stop the boat, but stopped when Uncle Pinchbeck fired the gun into one of the upper stairs above Jonathan's head. Uncle Pinchbeck wasn't kidding.

"I'm perfectly content with things the way they are. Your little friend is a fine navigator—she'll take us straight to them. In the meantime, sit down."

Jonathan slowly sat down and wracked his brain for ideas. Surely Katherine would come and check on him soon. And then what? She would be in danger of being shot, as well. He had to keep Uncle Pinchbeck distracted.

"I have to give you credit, Uncle," he said slowly, trying to lie like a professional. "Your plans for Treasure Island are very impressive."

Uncle Pinchbeck's eyebrows arched and he turned the flashlight away for a moment to reach into his coat pocket. He retrieved the missing papers. "Yes," he said slowly. "When it's done, it will be a historic resort without compare. My great, great, great grandfather would be proud of me."

Jonathan grimaced and shook his head. He seriously doubted Robert Louis Stevenson would approve.

He had to create some kind of distraction. If he could get up the stairs fast enough, he could close the cabin door and lock it. Uncle Pinchbeck, however, was not so easily fooled.

"I see you looking around everywhere," he said. "It's no use. I'll shoot you if you try to get away."

"Wouldn't that mess up your perfect plan?" Jonathan said sarcastically.

Uncle Pinchbeck grinned viciously, but said nothing. Instead, he reached around the gun to check the safety, and at that moment, the boat suddenly gave a tremendous lurch. The gun flew out of his hand and both uncle and nephew fell to the floor.

The flashlight rolled across the deck and came to a rest pointing at the wall. The room was bathed in darkness again.

Jonathan scrambled until he felt the icy coldness of the gun, then scurried for the stairs. Behind him, he could hear Uncle Pinchbeck cursing and crawling his way to the flashlight. Jonathan slam-med the cabin door shut and began looking for something to jam against it. Katherine appeared out of nowhere holding a gold key.

"This will help," she said, twisting it in the lock with a look of satisfaction.

"What happened?" Jonathan said, trying to catch his breath.

"I came down to check on you and saw the situation. I ran back up and intentionally put the boat aground, hoping it would distract your uncle long enough for you to get away."

Jonathan smiled and hugged her. "You're better than Jim Hawkins!" he said.

She backed away and pointed at the gun. "Careful, Jon. That thing is loaded."

"I know," he said, studying it as if it were some kind of dead animal. "But we may need it, and we can't leave it where Uncle Pinchbeck might get it. We've got to get my parents now, before the dogs get there."

"At least unload it," she said.

Jonathan fumbled until all of the shells were out, then shoved the bullets in one pocket, and the gun into the other. Below, they could hear Uncle Pinchbeck screaming threats at them.

"Come on! Let's go."

The boat was still in several feet of water, so they jumped into the blackness, not really trusting the depth until their feet hit the bottom. Then they waded ashore in the growing darkness away from the lights of the *Victory*.

The ran along the trail as fast as they could, pausing only when they neared the treasure site where the goons had been tied up. Strange sounds slowed them down.

"It sounds like an animal," Katherine said.

"No, it's someone grunting," Jonathan said.

They edged closer and discovered that the goons had escaped their bonds and were digging even more bars of silver up and setting them on a makeshift litter. There appeared to be at least two dozen already.

Clarence was directing Graham. "Come on, Graham, faster! We've got to hide this and get some more out to convince Pinchbeck!"

"I'm digging as fast as I can!" Graham whined.

"They're stealing the treasure," Katherine said.

Jonathan pulled her off the trail into the brush. "We don't have time—we have to get my parents."

They circled around, then continued on the trail until they reached the shack, which seemed unusu-ally quiet and deserted. They ran inside and dis-covered it empty.

"They're gone!"

Jonathan shook his head helplessly. The sound of barking dogs was in the distance.

"Come on," Katherine said, pulling him out of the shack into the clearing. "They couldn't have gone far."

As if on cue, a low whistle emanated from the undergrowth nearby. Mr. Cox emerged and waved them over.

"The dogs were getting too close. We buried all of our stuff here, so we can throw them off the scent for a while. We were just getting ready to leave."

"We have the *Victory*," Katherine said.

"And Uncle Pinchbeck with it."

The sound of the barking dogs grew closer, and men's voices could be heard encouraging them and whacking at the brush with machetes.

Mr. Cox nodded. "We've got to go now."

Jonathan's mother was drowsy from the effects of her illness, but could walk under her own power. With her pushed along by Jonathan's father, they rushed down the trail toward the treasure site, and then the *Victory*, as fast as they could. The sounds of the men and dogs faded back and forth, sometimes closer, and sometimes further away.

When they neared the treasure site again, Jonathan stopped them and took the gun out of his pocket.

His mother was shocked. "Jonathan! Put that thing down!"

"It's not loaded," he said quickly. "We had to

take it from Uncle Pinchbeck. We locked him on the boat. Listen to this, though. I have an idea."

Moments later, having reluctantly agreed, Mr. Cox emerged from the forest and yelled at the goons. They immediately looked up, Clarence auto-matically reaching for his own weapon on the ground nearby.

"Don't move!" Mr. Cox said. "Put your hands up very slowly." The goons cautiously complied. "Now, very slowly, pick up the litter and walk in front of me."

They hesitated until Mr. Cox took another step forward and released the safety catch. Then, they decided that doing what they were told was much safer.

Jonathan, Katherine, and Mrs. Cox followed behind Mr. Cox, who pointed the gun at the goons the whole time.

"Where are we going?" Graham asked, grunt-ing with exertion under the heavy load of silver bars he was carrying.

"Mr. Pinchbeck asked us to load this for him," Mr. Cox said.

Graham and Clarence exchanged a look but said nothing.

When they reached the Victory, it appeared that nothing had changed. It still sat quietly in the shal-low water, its running lights glowing brightly.

"How we gonna get this out there?" Clarence

said.

"You're not through carrying it yet," Mr. Cox replied, waving the gun. "Wade out to the boat and hoist it up."

"What if Uncle Pinchbeck is still on the ship?" Jonathan whispered. "Can't they just leave us here and take the silver?"

"You're right," Mr. Cox answered quietly. "You and I will go out with them, then come back for your mother and Katherine when the ship is secured."

Katherine nodded in agreement, trying to see of the tide had raised the ship up yet. She crouched down beside Mrs. Cox, who was catching her breath and looking a little worse for it after the hasty trek through the dank night air. Katherine returned the borrowed sweater to her.

Jonathan and his father followed the goons out to the *Victory*.

"This thing is too heavy!" Graham protested, his legs pumping through the deepening water.

"You're almost there—keep moving," Mr. Cox said, his voice unsympathetic.

"The cabin door is still closed, the way I left it," Jonathan said hopefully. Perhaps Uncle Pinchbeck was still confined there.

"I hope he is there," Mr. Cox said, anger rising in his voice. "There are some things that need said."

When they were beside the ship, Jonathan and his father climbed aboard and lowered a rope for the goons to aid in their task of loading the treasure. Then, both Jonathan and his father cautiously approached the cabin door. Mr. Cox still held the gun.

"Let me go first," he said to Jonathan.

They cautiously started down the darkened steps. There was no sign of activity below. Outside, the goons were arguing about who was lifting the most.

"He's not—" Jonathan started to say, but he never completed the sentence. A cold, hard (well-tailored) arm reached around his mouth and jerked him sideways. Jonathan felt something cold against his cheek.

"Freeze, Lawrence, or you'll never see your son again!"

Mr. Cox wheeled around just as the light clicked on to reveal Uncle Pinchbeck. Jonathan thought about struggling, but the coldness of the gun barrel on his cheek dissuaded him.

"Drop it or he'll get hurt!"

Jonathan watched his father slowly lower his arm and place the pistol on the floor. "I should have known you'd have another gun, Frank. That's the only way people like you can get what they want."

Uncle Pinchbeck laughed, inadvertently forcing the gun to jiggle against Jonathan's face. "Oh, you're funny, Lawrence. I have as much claim to this island as Hillary does, although it'll probably take a lawyer to convince you of that."

"Let Jon go," Mr. Cox said. "He has nothing to do with this."

Uncle Pinchbeck pressed the gun even tighter and Jonathan winced. "You're wrong again! He's the reason I'm standing here right now, wasting precious time! If he'd never come to this island, none of this ever would have happened!"

"Yes, and Hillary and I would have died, and the whole thing would have been forgotten." Mr. Cox said, completing the thought. "Right? No one would have asked any questions, would they?"

Uncle Pinchbeck seemed to falter for a second. "I didn't really try to hurt anyone..." he said slowly.

"You didn't? The airport records at Martinkey will probably have something to say about that, won't they? And I'm sure the dogs you've sent out were to find us—not hurt us. German Shepherds are good tracking dogs, aren't they? And I'm sure that you didn't stock this island with constrictors and wildcats just to keep people away, did you? Actually, I'd say you've tried to hurt people, Frank."

Jonathan could feel his uncle's arm shaking, and it made him nervous. What if he shot Jonathan accidentally? What if his dad made Uncle Pinch-beck so mad that he wanted to shoot Jonathan?

"I haven't done anything wrong," Uncle Pinch-beck insisted. "Everything has been good business practice! You just don't understand business! You never have."

Mr. Cox took one step toward them. "Does good business practice include the illegal mining of rutile, or the "goods" as you put it, so you can keep that fat contract with the government?"

Uncle Pinchbeck gasped and backed up to the first step, still clutching Jonathan tightly. "How did you find out about the submarines?"

Mr. Cox shook his head. "It doesn't matter. I also found out that you stole those papers from Hillary, had them copied, then tried to replace them so no one would suspect they had ever been missing."

Uncle Pinchbeck pulled the gun away from Jonathan's face and now pointed it at Jonathan's father. Rage covered the lines of his face. "Those papers were as much mine as hers! Could I help it she found them first, then wouldn't share them with me?"

"What about Grandfather Osbourne's house and land?" Mr. Cox continued, taking another step toward Uncle Pinchbeck, "And then your sudden name change on the eve of a big lawsuit? All in all, Frank, your record speaks for itself. You're a crook, and worse yet, you're an inept one."

Uncle Pinchbeck's face turned beet red and he finally seemed to muster the courage to focus. He stepped forward, instead of backwards, not just aiming the gun, but fingering the trigger.

"I don't have to listen to this," Uncle Pinchbeck said. "This is outrageous and untrue! I never have trusted you, Lawrence. My sister deserved so much more than what your meager salary provides... If she were here now, she'd agree with me!"

Jonathan tensed, ready to leap and knock the gun away, when another voice from the top of the stairs intervened.

"Don't be so sure, Frank!"

Hillary Cox struggled down the stairs with Katherine trailing behind her, still looking sickly and tired, but her eyes were filled with fire. "How dare you say these things! You've taken advantage of me, and worse yet, of our own grandfather! What would he have said about this kind of behavior?"

Uncle Pinchbeck's eyes fell to the floor. Jonathan prepared himself once more to leap, and again, his mother forestalled him.

"Put that gun down, Frank. We've all had a

long night. Put it down now!"

Uncle Pinchbeck slowly put the gun on the floor and Jonathan immediately scooped it up. He opened the chamber to unload it and found it empty. "It's not loaded!"

Mr. Cox strode over to look at the gun and concurred with Jonathan.

"You see?" Uncle Pinchbeck said, "I wouldn't really have hurt him."

Mr. Cox started to say something, but Jonathan's mother motioned for him to remain silent.

"Come on, Frank. Go in the kitchen and tell me why this has all happened. You've got some explaining to do. You come in the kitchen and I'll make you something to drink. Then we'll talk about what to do at Martinkey. It's not too late to do the right thing."

Uncle Pinchbeck drew up suddenly. "Martinkey? What are you talking about?"

Katherine proudly stepped down the last stair and smiled broadly. "The tide came in and we were starting to drift. Mrs. Cox and I took the liberty of setting a course for Martinkey."

Uncle Pinchbeck closed his eyes, his expression indicating that, finally, he was ready to concede defeat.

"What about those goons?" Mr. Cox said Katherine.

Uncle Pinchbeck frowned and interrupted.

"Clarence and Graham were with you? What were they doing? Are they here?" There was a slight degree of hope in his voice, as if maybe the battle could be started up again with the numbers more even.

"Oh, no," Katherine said, smiling at Uncle Pinchbeck. "We marooned them back on the island with the animals. They'll have to fend for themselves against Flint's ghost."

"What do you mean?" Uncle Pinchbeck said slowly.

"I mean," Katherine said, still grinning, "that Flint's treasure is topside, and he's not going to be happy about seeing it taken. He'll have to content himself with Clarence and Graham to haunt."

Uncle Pinchbeck's lips pursed, then without another word, he moved into the kitchen, with Mrs. Cox pushing him along like a nanny. Mr. Cox took both guns and locked them up in the desk, placing the key in his pocket.

Then he smiled at Jonathan and Katherine. "I guess I should be thanking both of you..."

Jonathan smiled and shook Katherine's hand. "Good job, partner."

"...However," Mr. Cox continued, "there is this little matter of the treasure.

Jonathan waited, barely able to contain himself. Katherine squirmed beside him.

"My idea is that we should divide it fifty-fifty and set up two college funds. What do you think?"

Jonathan turned to Katherine, but he already knew what the answer would be.

Chapter 17

SEVERAL WEEKS later, Katherine and Jonathan were back in rural Georgia, mending her father's fishing nets. The late summer sunshine was warm and reassuring, and a light breeze blew in the faint smell of salt-water and fish. It was perfect (even though summer break was almost over).

Katherine was wearing her usual old clothes, but it was by choice this time, Jonathan knew. Her new clothes were for school or going to town. Her father's boat, too, looked brand new because, in fact, it was brand new. The money from the bar sil-ver had exceeded their expectations several times.

"Money isn't everything, you know," Katherine said, as if reading Jonathan's thoughts.

He shrugged. "I know. What makes you think I worship money?"

"I don't think you do, but it seems to me like a lot of people have money and it doesn't do them a bit of good as far as happiness is concerned. Your uncle is the perfect example."

"You're right about that. It's hard to enjoy

your money if you're in jail." Jonathan couldn't help smiling broadly.

Katherine's face puckered up like it did when she was about to say something unpleasant. Jonathan prepared himself.

"And your parents, too," she said slowly. "It's wonderful that they're alive and well, but—"

"But what?"

"Well, the treasure hasn't really brought them happiness, has it?"

Jonathan put down the bone needle and section of net he was working on and stared off into the ocean thoughtfully. Katherine was right, as usual, but probably not for all the right reasons.

"Everything we do comes at a price," he said. "But my parents aren't doing this for happiness anymore. They're doing it because it's the right thing. The court battle will probably last years, knowing how Uncle Pinchbeck's lawyers work. They have an obligation that might be a little unpleasant. It's just like us—did we ever stop to think what we were putting Longfellow and your father through when we disappeared? But we did it any-way. My parents will make sure the island is taken care of."

"No," she said quickly, "that's not what I mean. You're still talking about money, or material goals. I mean beyond that."

Jonathan paused. This time, Katherine had

gone into territory that he was unfamiliar with. He laughed, then threw his hands up helplessly.

"My parents are safe; the island will be preserved as a memorial to Robert Louis Stevenson; we both have money for college and then some; my uncle is going to jail; your father has a new boat—what am I missing here? I don't get it!"

She shook her head again, her face full of freckles and a growing smile.

"You still don't get it?"

Jonathan didn't know what to do, and before he could think of anything, stupid or otherwise, Katherine leaned over and kissed him on the cheek. It instantly reminded him of the electric feeling on the *Victory* when they had held hands and spotted the Treasure Island for the first time.

"Don't ever forget, Jonathan Cox, what your real treasures are."

There was no doubt about it—no amount of money or treasure would spoil Katherine.

They laughed together, and enjoyed what was probably the best day of their lives. Good old great, great, great, great, granddad would have been proud of them, Jonathan decided. And Jim Haw-kins, too. Maybe even Long John!

HISTORICAL NOTE: Robert Louis Stevenson did not have any children of his own, although he did have a stepson through marriage.

In the original Treasure Island, Jim Hawkins does indeed report that the bar silver, some jewels, and the arms cache were left behind because the Hispaniola was already overfilled. He also points out that he never wants to return to the terrible island.

There do remain, even in 1999, many remote, uncharted, unexplored islands in the Atlantic Ocean.

~ *The End* ~

Jack Trammell

Author Jack Trammell's credits include "The Saints Departed", a highly recommended historical novel, "Appalachian Dreams," a collection of new and previously published poems, and two novels "Gray," and "Coming Home," serialized on the Fiction Network. He has published numerous poems, a novella, and non-fiction articles in magazines like "America's Civil War," "Instructor Magazine," "Linn's Stamp News," etc. His current projects include a Civil War novel set in his native state of Kentucky, and another collection of poetry.

Jack lives in central Virginia with his wife and three children. His students helped him draft and edit "Return to Treasure Island."

Lightning Source UK Ltd.
Milton Keynes UK
UKOW051320110112

185179UK00001B/14/A